Gianna Must Have Realized
He Had No Intention Of Leaving.

With a sigh of irritation, she walked to her closet, flinging open the door and disappearing inside. Curious, he followed.

"Madre di Dio," Constantine murmured faintly.

"I don't want to hear a word about it," she retorted, her back to him.

He caught the defensive edge in her voice. "Just out of curiosity, how many pairs of shoes do you own?"

Gianna turned, clutching a pair of heels. "Not enough. They're not all mine. Some of them are Francesca's. We discovered a while back that we both wear identical sizes."

Constantine folded his arms across his chest. "Should I assume that if some of these are hers, she has some of yours?"

"That's none of your business," she muttered.

"It will be when we marry."

She held up a hand. "Okay, stop right there. There is no 'when.' There is only a very shaky 'maybe.'"

Dear Reader,

It has been such a pleasure to write about the Dante family romances, to see each member succumb to The Inferno, that all-consuming blaze of heat and electricity that a Dante experiences when he or she first touches their soul mate. Now it's Gianna's turn, and she has an even more difficult path to happily-ever-after than any of her brothers or cousins.

You may remember meeting the hero, Constantine Romano, in *Dante's Contract Marriage,* where Lazz Dante and Ariana Romano met for the first time while exchanging their wedding vows. Constantine is Ariana's brother, and apparently that infamous wedding day saw more than one Romano Infernoed!

But Constantine Romano isn't a man easily manipulated, not even by The Inferno. He is a man who makes his own decisions in life and controls his own destiny. And he isn't happy to discover that control taken away from him by either The Inferno or the woman on the other side of that first, electric touch—Gianna Dante.

I hope you enjoy discovering how Gianna's love story plays out. But stay tuned. Although this is the final book in the current quartet, it may not be the final tale in *The Dante Legacy.* Read on to discover why!

Warmly,

Day Leclaire

DAY LECLAIRE

DANTE'S HONOR-BOUND HUSBAND

♦ **Harlequin**®

Desire

4.75

Recycling programs
for this product may
not exist in your area.

ISBN-13: 978-0-373-73100-8

DANTE'S HONOR-BOUND HUSBAND

Copyright © 2011 by Day Totton Smith

www.Harlequin.com

Printed in U.S.A.

main

Books by Day Leclaire

Desire

DAY LECLAIRE

USA TODAY bestselling author Day Leclaire is described by Harlequin Books as "one of our most popular writers ever!" Day's tremendous worldwide popularity has made her a member of Harlequin's "Five Star Club," with sales of well over five million books. She is a three-time winner of both a Colorado Award of Excellence and a Golden Quill Award. She's won *RT Book Reviews* Career Achievement and Love and Laughter Awards, a Holt Medallion and a Booksellers' Best Award. She has also received an impressive ten nominations for the prestigious Romance Writers of America's RITA® Award.

Day's romances touch the heart and make you care about her characters as much as she does. In Day's own words, "I adore writing romances, and can't think of a better way to spend each day." For more information, visit Day on her website, www.dayleclaire.com.

To Mary-Theresa Hussey.
An absolutely brilliant editor.
A kind and generous person.
As always, it's been such a delight working with you.
Thank you for making my books more.

Prologue

"Don't go."

Constantine Romano closed his eyes and fought for control. "I have no choice." His integrity, his honor as a Romano, everything that made him a man demanded he leave.

"Then let me go with you." Gianna Dante lifted her gaze to his, her striking jade-green eyes bright with tears, her hair a glorious tumble of autumn-gold and brown. "I can help you."

Her plea pushed him to the limit of his self-control, where he teetered between honor and caving to the intensity of his need to make her his. He fought to resist and couldn't, not entirely. He cupped her face and snatched a kiss. Took another, then sank in. God, she was amazing. Stunning. Intelligent. Graceful. Possessing a femininity that left him desperate with longing.

They'd met when his sister, Ariana, had married Gianna's

cousin, Lazz. The moment he'd taken her hand in his, he'd been hit by an overwhelming flame of desire. A physical flash and burn that had shocked him to the core with its all-encompassing depth and strength and power. In that instant, every other thought and emotion had ceased to exist except for a cascade of urgent directives....

Take her.

Make her his.

Put his stamp on her in every and any way possible.

"I want you to come with me, even though I don't understand any of this," he admitted. Didn't understand how he could want so fast and so deeply. How a single weekend with her could make him so certain that she was the only one for him. "How is it possible that in just a few short days I know that you're the woman I want to spend the rest of my life with?"

Her gaze dropped and for a split second she looked almost guilty. Though what she had to feel guilty about, he couldn't imagine. It wasn't her fault that he'd been overwhelmed with this desperate need to possess her. More than anything he wanted to take her to his bed, but he knew, even without her telling him, that she'd never been with a man before. And if he couldn't put his ring on her finger, he refused to dishonor either of them—or their families—by making love to her. Not until he could afford to offer marriage.

"I didn't expect to feel such intense desire, either," she confessed. Her gaze flitted upward, filled with heartbreak. "Please, Constantine. I don't want you to leave."

He tugged her closer and allowed their bodies to collide and meld once again. "I don't want to leave, either, *piccola*. But until I have something more to offer than my name, I must return home to Italy."

"For how long?"

A good question. Too bad it was one he couldn't answer.

"Until I get my restoration business up and running. Until I can afford a wife and have the means to support her." He stopped her when she would have argued, stopped her in the most delicious way possible. "Don't, Gianna. Don't ask me to compromise my values. I'll return as soon as I can. And when I do, I'll be in the position to offer you marriage. To put my ring on your finger. This I swear on my family name."

He could see endless arguments building, arguments she controlled and suppressed, impressing the hell out of him. "I'll wait. You know I'll wait. And in the meantime, we can talk on the phone." Her chin quivered, but she used a considerable amount of will to steady it. "And there's always email. I'll fly over as often as I can. Maybe you can visit during holidays."

Every word she uttered made it more and more difficult. Nearly impossible. He gathered her hands in his. "Listen to me, Gianna… In order to get back to you as soon as possible, I must focus on work. Every minute of every day. It's the only way to make it happen quickly."

A frown formed between her brows. "What are you saying?"

"I'm saying that you're a distraction. I'm saying if you're with me or come to visit or if we are constantly calling one another or emailing, I won't be able to give my full attention to my business. It's at a critical point right now. The only way I can return to you in the least amount of time is if I give one hundred percent of my time and attention to Romano Restoration."

Her breath hitched. "Oh, no. Constantine, you can't mean it. No phone calls? Not even emails?"

She was killing him by inches. He closed his eyes so he wouldn't cave while everything within him insisted he do just that. "Please understand, *amore*. Please trust me."

A tear escaped, but she swept it away. Determination filled her expression. "Okay, Constantine, we'll do this your way. For now." Her eyes glittered with emotion. "But you come back. Soon," she ordered fiercely.

"As soon as I can," he promised.

And then he left her. He forced himself not to look back, even though it was one of the most difficult things he'd ever done. With every step he took, he felt that odd connection that joined them. Felt it compelling him to return to her arms, urging him to take what was his. He'd never experienced anything like it. Oh, he'd return to her. He had no choice. But it would be on his terms.

Soon. Dear God, just let it be soon.

Gianna watched Constantine walk away until the tears blurring her eyes made it impossible to see any longer. Should she have told him? Had she made a mistake not explaining about The Inferno—the family "blessing" that sparked between a man and a woman whenever a Dante first touched his or her soul mate? Perhaps. As for keeping it a secret... Well, she had her reasons, not that he'd appreciate them once he discovered the truth behind their odd connection.

She closed her eyes, accepting the hand fate had dealt her. The Inferno had struck almost all of her other Dante relatives...all of her *male* Dante relatives the first time they met the women who were their soul mates. As the lone female Dante, no one knew whether it was even possible for her to experience The Inferno. She'd learned the answer to that question when she and Constantine first touched. She could and she did. Unfortunately the secret she'd learned about The Inferno hadn't altered that basic fact.

But she'd been afraid to explain the Dantes' odd...condition...to Constantine. In the short time she'd known him, she'd realized he was a man who preferred to govern his own destiny, to control his world and those in it. Once he discovered that The Inferno drove the desire and passion he felt, would he be compelled to fight it? They'd had too little time together to know for certain. Until she could be sure, it would remain her little secret.

Now all she could do was wait for Constantine's return. Wait and see if The Inferno was real…or an illusion. If her family had been correct in their beliefs about it…or if the secret she'd uncovered all those years ago was the real truth. Only time would tell.

Soon. Dear God, just let it be soon.

One

He'd returned.

Constantine Romano entered the room as though he owned the place. But then, he possessed the sort of presence bred into the very essence of the man. The sort of presence that went with his aristocratic name and stunning bone structure and taut, muscular body. He wore his hair longer than before, the ebony curls and fierce black eyes summoning images of dangerous pirates and ferocious duels of honor. Beneath that elegant exterior smoldered a man of action, who would risk everything, dare all and take whatever he wanted.

And he wanted her.

Gianna Dante shuddered, struggling to gather up her self-control. She'd have to face him and soon. Since their first meeting, over a year and a half ago, a lot had changed. Though she now doubted Constantine had experienced The Inferno during that unforgettable weekend they'd shared,

The Inferno had given him an uncanny knack for sensing her presence. That much she remembered. Any second he'd hone in on her and she'd darn well better be prepared.

"Gianna? Would you care to check the display?"

It took her a moment to switch gears and focus on work. Tomorrow marked Dantes' Midsummer Night's gala and a million details remained, each requiring her immediate attention. As Dantes' event coordinator, she took care of everything from the catering to the decorations to the displays to the invitations. Fortunately she had an excellent assistant who was every bit as detail-oriented as she was herself.

"Thank you, Tara. I'll be right there."

Considering that Constantine stood between her and the display in question, she might as well get the coming confrontation over with. She took a deep breath. No big deal, she tried to tell herself. The feelings she'd experienced that long-ago weekend had faded over the ensuing months, months which had ticked by with excruciating slowness. The legendary Dante Inferno, that amazing sensation of volcanic fire that erupted when he'd taken her hand in his had quieted, drifting into dormancy. She could handle this.

She'd simply make it clear to him that she'd moved on.

Gianna started across Dantes' ballroom toward him, thankful that by some blessing of fate she'd chosen to wear one of her "killer" outfits. The vibrant red jacket and tight, short skirt showed off her figure to its best advantage, and the mile-high open-toe heels were the perfect showcase for the gorgeous legs she'd inherited from her equally gorgeous mother. Her hair was longer than the last time she'd seen him, flowing in heavy, layered curls to the middle of her back.

Let him look. Let him want. And let him regret.

She hadn't traversed more than a half dozen steps before Constantine stilled with abrupt predatory awareness. His head turned in her direction and his ink-dark eyes glittered with unmistakable intent. He came for her, moving with a focused grace that almost sent her fleeing in the opposite direction. To her shock, he didn't stop when he reached her, but kept coming. He invaded her space and swept her into his arms. Then, with her name on his lips and a smothered protest on hers, he kissed her.

He devoured her, the kiss one of blatant possession, branding her with a mark of ownership that in any other situation she'd have fought with every ounce of her strength. Instead all thought of resistance melted beneath the blazing heat and she sank inward, opening herself to him. He tasted like ambrosia combined with a hint of spice and topped with a hard, masculine kick. It utterly devastated her senses, along with every scrap of practicality.

It had been so incredibly long since they last touched— nineteen months, five days, eight hours and a handful of minutes. Desire in the form of The Inferno had exploded between them at that first touch. Then after a single weekend of bliss, he'd left her.

Despair vied with an incandescent joy. His coming now, after all this time was too little, too late. Why now? Why, when she'd finally come to terms with the impossibility of knowing the sort of Inferno love affair that everyone else in her family possessed, had Constantine chosen this moment to return?

It wasn't fair.

"Stop," she managed to protest. "This is wrong."

How could she tell him? How could she say the words that threatened to break her heart? She'd moved on. She'd found someone else.

He finally picked up on her signals and pulled back a

few precious inches. "Stop?" He captivated her with a single smile. "What are you talking about, *piccola?* After all this time, we're together again. How could something so incredibly right possibly be wrong?"

She slipped free of his embrace and tugged at the bottom of her jacket to straighten it. Somehow the first two buttons had come undone revealing a tantalizing flash of black lace. She did her best to neaten all the various bits and pieces he'd rumpled. She moistened her lips, aware he'd kissed every bit of lipstick from them.

"It's good to see you, Constantine," she said with polite formality.

He froze. "Good to see me?" he repeated softly.

She flinched at the dangerous tone, one infused with the warmth of his Tuscan home, yet chilled with the ice of his displeasure. This was going to be far more difficult than she'd anticipated. "Are you here on business? I hope you'll take a few minutes to drop by my grandparents before you return to Italy." She offered a friendly smile to cover up her nervous chatter. "They were asking after you the other day."

"Don't you understand? I've relocated to San Francisco."

No. No, no, *no!* It wasn't fair. Not now, after all this time. Praying that none of her thoughts were echoed in her expression, she kept her smile pinned in place, a careless, nonchalant one that made it clear that his news didn't make the least difference to her. "Congratulations."

He caught her chin in the palm of his hand and tipped her face up to his. "Is that all you have to say to me? Congratulations?"

Her smile faded along with all attempts at concealing her emotions. Pain and anger ripped through her and she jerked back from his touch, her impetuous nature decimating her common sense. "What do you want from me, Constantine?" she demanded, the question escaping in a low, fierce undertone. "It's been nearly two years. I've moved on. I suggest you do the same."

His head jerked back as though she'd slapped him. "Moved on?" His accent thickened, deepened. "What does this mean…moved on?"

She dismissed the question with a sweep of her hand. "Don't give me that. You understand idiomatic English just fine. It means precisely what you think it means."

"There is someone else?"

"Yes, Constantine. There *is* someone else." For the first time, Gianna realized they were the center of all eyes and warmth swept across her cheekbones. "Now, if you'll excuse me, I have work to do if I'm going to get this place ready for tomorrow's gala."

She'd never seen him look so hard or distant. He inclined his head in a regal manner. "Please. Do not let me get in your way."

Gathering up her emotions and stuffing them behind an equally regal manner, she spun on her heel and crossed to the nearest display case. She stared blindly at the contents. She wasn't the one who cut ties or ended their relationship prematurely, she reminded herself. He'd given her a handful of amazing days when they first met and then walked away from what might have been. The fact that he'd been able to do that solidified her suspicions about The Inferno. Her family didn't know the entire truth about the family "blessing." But she did. She'd been thirteen years old when she'd overheard how it really worked.

As for Constantine… If he'd experienced the depth of desire she had, he managed to control it well all this time. To dismiss it while he took care of more important business. Until they'd met she'd thought it impossible to fall in love so completely. She thought Constantine had fallen in love with her, as well. Foolish of her, Gianna now realized. She'd spent all these endless months overwhelmed by a cascade of passionate emotions. Emotions that—had he shared them—should have made him incapable of leaving her. Clearly he didn't share a damn thing.

She'd suffered while he'd walked away.

That left her with a single, logical and thoroughly devastating conclusion. He didn't love her. Not really. And that forced her to face an agonizing realization. If she surrendered to him now, he'd own her body and soul. But what would she possess? A man capable of picking her up and setting her aside whenever he wished. She couldn't live like that. She *refused* to live like that.

For her, for whatever reason, the burn of The Inferno only went one way. Otherwise, Constantine wouldn't have left her. Otherwise, he couldn't have stayed away for so long or curtailed all communication. Well, if he could turn off The Inferno, so could she, though she'd never learned that portion of the secret. Somehow. Someway. Even if it killed her, she'd put an end to it. She closed her eyes against the tears pressing for release.

God, she loved him.

Figlio di puttana! Constantine watched Gianna walk away. Bitter frustration ate at him. Nineteen damn months. For nineteen months, five days, eight hours and a handful of minutes he'd fought and clawed to get his fledgling business, Romano Restoration, off the ground and soaring so that he could emigrate to the United States and establish a stronghold in San Francisco. All to provide Gianna with more than a name when he asked her to marry him. And now that his company had taken off and he was in a position to support a wife, the only woman he wanted was walking away with a hip-swinging stride that knocked every last brain cell off-line.

Another man! His hands collapsed into fists. *How could she?* He'd promised he'd return the instant he could provide for her, and she'd agreed to wait. For nearly two years he'd worked endless days and nights to make that happen. How could she turn her back on what they had? What they could have? Didn't she feel it, that ferocious wildfire that exploded into flames whenever they were in the same room together?

He stared down at his balled hands and it took every ounce of resolve to ignore the relentless itch centered in the palm of his right hand. It was an itch that had flared to life the first moment Gianna Dante had slipped her fine-boned hand into his, and it had continued over the course of the ensuing months, no matter how much distance separated them.

Constantine knew what it was. Though Gianna had neglected to explain what she'd done to him—a lengthy and pointed discussion for another time—his sister, Ariana, had described it in graphic detail after her husband, Lazz, had Infernoed her when they'd first joined hands at the altar on their wedding day. Those damned Dantes and their damnable Inferno. It wasn't enough that they'd used it to overpower his sister. That wasn't good enough for them. Hell, no. For some reason, the sole Dante female had chosen him for her mate, had used The Inferno to steal every last crumb of his own self-control. Ever since that day he'd been trapped with no hope of escape other than to surrender to its demands.

And now, he couldn't even do that because Gianna had "moved on." He wanted to roar in outrage. Not a chance in hell would he let her get away with it. She'd soon discover that she couldn't move on, up, down, or sideways without his being right there waiting for her. Whoever she'd chosen to infect with The Inferno this time around was out of luck.

No matter what it took, no matter whether she faced her fate willingly or otherwise, he intended to claim Gianna Dante for his own. The Inferno might have caused him to lose his legendary control, but marriage to her would allow him to regain it. Once he had his ring on her finger and her delightful curves in his bed, this hideous need would ease and he'd be able to wield it as *he* saw fit. Until then... He stared at her broodingly.

God, he wanted her.

"Did you hear the news?" Elia Dante asked. She lounged in a chair outside the dressing rooms of a snazzy little boutique called Sinfully Delicious. "No, Gianna. Not the salmon. Go with the bronze halter gown. It complements your eyes better than the other one."

Gianna held up one gown, then the other, before nodding in agreement. Though why she bothered to compare the two, she didn't know. When it came to fashion, her mother was infallible. "What news?"

Elia took a delicate sip from a tiny cup of espresso before announcing, "Constantine Romano has moved to San Francisco. He opens the doors to Romano Restoration any day now. Apparently he organized the transition all the way from Italy."

Gianna stiffened, grateful she had her back turned to her mother. She should have anticipated this. Foolish of her not to, all things considered. "That's rather unexpected, isn't it?"

"Do you think so?" Elia asked softly. "Somehow he's gotten his entire operation up and running without any of us being the wiser." She lifted a delicate eyebrow. "I'm guessing as a surprise for a certain someone?"

Gianna sighed. Her mother was the only person who knew what she'd experienced when she and Constantine first met. She'd been very careful to keep it from everyone else, knowing her family would interfere if they knew. "Yes, Mamma, it is. What we had, or rather, what I thought we had ended a long time ago."

"The Inferno doesn't end, *chiacchierona*."

"Maybe it does."

Gianna swung around to face her mother. What would Elia say if she knew the whole truth about The Inferno? If she'd heard what Gianna had when Uncle Dominic explained the facts to Aunt Laura? Or watched what he'd done to rid them both of The Inferno? She'd never dared tell anyone, terrified that she'd see other relationships ruined as a result of her revelation. If the rest of her family believed in The Inferno with all their hearts, maybe they'd never discover what her aunt and uncle had...

That The Inferno *wasn't* forever.

Gianna hesitated, still unwilling to tell her mother the entire truth. She chose her words with care. "Maybe it's different because I'm a woman instead of a man," she suggested. "Maybe it only went one way and he doesn't feel what I do."

"If that were so, Constantine wouldn't be here."

"Maybe I can take The Inferno back," she dared to suggest.

Elia simply laughed. "That's not possible. The Inferno is forever."

Oh, but it wasn't. Gianna set her chin. "It doesn't matter if Constantine is here now. It's too late."

A mother's wisdom gleamed in Elia's dark eyes. "That's your pride speaking, not your heart."

"I've moved on," Gianna insisted, wincing at the defensive edge underscoring her words. "I'm dating David d'Angelo now."

"Well, he is Italian...like Constantine," her mother conceded. "And comes from a good Fiorentini family, though not one anywhere near as noble as the Romanos."

"Maybe not, but they're respected bankers."

The family was even receiving some sort of banking award in another few months. As for David, he possessed stunning good looks. Granted, they were more classical than swashbuckling. More attractive even than her brother, Rafe, whom the family called the "pretty Dante." Not that David could help his looks.

As for his personality, he couldn't be nicer. Even if Primo had muttered *untuoso* under his breath, which had bothered Gianna no end since she didn't consider David the least unctuous. Nonna adored him, which counted for a lot. David was intelligent, respectful and amusing, despite possessing the faintest air of entitlement.

And if he hadn't told her he was Italian by birth, she'd never have guessed it by his accent, perhaps as a result of his studying abroad for so many years. Now that she thought about it, other than his intelligence he was as different from Constantine as a bird of paradise from a panther.

"David's not like Constantine," Elia murmured, the comment an uncomfortable echo of Gianna's own thoughts.

"He is in some ways," she argued. "But the important point here is that I like him very much. That's all that matters, right?"

Elia made a face and set her cup and saucer aside. "*Like*. What an insipid word. Would you really trade an earth-shattering passion for a tepid 'like'?"

"It's safer," Gianna whispered.

Safer not to surrender to the dangerous emotions flaring back to life. Safer not to allow the more impetuous side of her nature free rein. Safer to like a nice guy than to love someone as dangerous to her emotional stability as Constantine Romano.

"I spoke to Ariana about the situation."

Uh-oh. "She and Lazz are still in Italy?" Gianna asked, hoping to turn the conversation in a new direction. No doubt a wasted effort.

"Yes. For another two months." Sure enough, her mother lasered back to her point. "According to her, Constantine's come back for you."

"His sister is a romantic. The Inferno has a way of doing that to you. I guarantee that before she met Lazz she was the most pragmatic of people." Gianna made a face in the mirror. "That's what The Inferno does to people. It messes with them."

"Mmm." The sound was one of delighted agreement. "With luck you will soon discover yourself in the middle of your own Inferno mess."

The comment contained a reminiscent tone and Gianna suspected her mother was recalling when she'd first fallen in love with Gianna's father, Alessandro. Though her parents' relationship could be tumultuous on occasion, there'd never been a doubt in her mind that they shared a white-hot passion, as well as being utterly devoted to each other.

"No, thanks, Mamma. I think I'll stick with David."

"I'm sure Constantine will try to change your mind about that." Elia paused for a beat, before adding, "And I suspect, you hope he'll succeed."

Since Gianna couldn't think of a response to that painful bit of homespun truth, she set the salmon gown aside and carried the bronze confection to the front desk. If only... came the wistful thought. If only The Inferno had worked as well between her and Constantine instead of backfiring so badly. Maybe she'd be sitting in a chair with that delicious smile on her face, lost in memories of endless days and nights filled with an eternal love.

If only.

As always, David arrived right on time. He looked spectacular in his tux, the light brown hair and turquoise eyes he'd inherited from the northern branch of the d'Angelo family giving him a movie-star sheen. It wasn't a coincidence that his coloring was the complete opposite of Constantine's. If he'd possessed hair as dark as night and eyes like jet, she'd never have agreed to go out with him the first time he'd asked. In fact, she hadn't. It had taken a full three months of patient persistence before she'd caved to his barrage of invitations.

He greeted her with a slow, easy kiss that didn't come close to impacting the way Constantine's had. If she were perfectly honest with herself, his kisses left her cold. No doubt she could thank The Inferno for that unfortunate wrinkle. She'd hoped—heaven help her but she'd hoped—that she'd been mistaken about what she'd felt when she and Constantine first touched. That at some point she'd begin to feel a modicum of that sort of desire for David. It was possible, regardless of what her relatives thought.

If their embraces lacked a certain spark, David never seemed to notice. And sure enough, he didn't this time, either. Perhaps he wasn't in the position to make the sort of comparison she could. He pulled back and studied her, his gaze warming in appreciation. He gestured toward her hair and gown. "You look stunning, Gia."

"Thanks," she said.

Aware of the tepidness of her response, she gave him an impulsive hug. What was wrong with her? David was drop-dead gorgeous. He'd made it clear that he wanted her, that his intentions were both honorable and serious—his words, which she found quite endearing. Regardless of how endearing, she just couldn't bring herself to take their relationship to the next level. And now that Constantine had returned…

No! She wouldn't go there. Couldn't. Constantine had made his feelings all too clear months ago when he'd left her. When he'd proved beyond a shadow of a doubt that The Inferno hadn't taken root with him the way it had with her. She'd moved on, and the man she'd chosen stood in front of her. David was everything she could ask for. A dedicated banker in international finance with a bright future ahead of him. A physique that left women drooling. And a calm, practical nature that balanced her more passionate, impulsive one. Maybe The Inferno would strike later in their relationship.

"Ready?" David asked.

"All set."

"Will the entire family be there?" The question held a certain edginess that had her wincing. David often found her family a bit overwhelming. "Will I finally get to meet Lazz and Ariana, or are they still in Italy?"

The question caught her by surprise. But then, he'd acknowledged a distant, passing acquaintance with the Romanos, so maybe it wasn't all that odd. "They're still on a working holiday for another couple months."

"A shame," he murmured, though she suspected a certain insincerity in the comment.

After locking the door of her elegant row house with its pretty gingerbread trim, they crossed to his Jaguar. As always, he opened the door for her, his courtesy an innate part of his personality. They drove to Dantes' corporate office building, chatting about inconsequential matters along the way. They'd almost reached their destination when David steered the conversation into more turbulent waters.

"I have to fly out to New York next week for a meeting," he announced after a momentary silence. He flashed her a quick grin. "A very boring meeting."

He'd mentioned the trip the previous week. "I understand." She spared him a sympathetic glance. "How long will you be gone this time?"

"Four days. Friday through Monday."

"Well, that's not too bad. And at least it isn't overseas."

"No, it's not." He pulled up to a red light and spared her a brief, meaningful glance that didn't sink in until he added, "I'd like you to come with me. My business won't take long. This particular meeting is more of a formality than anything else."

"Oh, I don't know, David," she began.

The light turned green and he continued through the intersection. "I'm not finished." A single glance at the determined set of his jaw and she fell silent. "I was thinking we'd get a suite at the Ritz."

The offer came so out of the blue that it took her a moment to switch gears. "The Ritz?" Wow. Then the rest of his comment filtered through. "Wait a minute. Do you mean… share a suite?"

"I mean a romantic weekend." His mouth compressed. "As in, no family breathing down our necks."

Gianna stiffened and she swiveled in her seat. "You feel as though my family is breathing down our necks?" she asked, excruciatingly polite.

He didn't take notice of the warning in her voice. "In a word, yes. You're twenty-five, Gianna. We've known each other for six months, been dating for three, but you're still holding me at arm's length."

"And you think my family's to blame for that?"

He still didn't seem to realize that he'd wandered onto extremely thin ice. How could he have dated her for even a week and not picked up on the fact that family meant everything to her? With the Dantes, family came first and foremost, just as she thought it must with the d'Angelos, despite David's more cosmopolitan lifestyle. *La famiglia,* right?

That also extended beyond blood ties. There was nothing the Dantes loved better than finding someone new to add to the fold. If David weren't so suspicious of their intent, right down to insisting that they keep their relationship on the down low until the past month when he'd finally agreed to be introduced to everyone, he'd have discovered that for himself. But for some reason, David's attitude caused her family to hold him at a cool, polite distance, except for her Nonna.

She saw the Dantes' corporate headquarters come in to sight. "I don't blame your family for the way you've held me at arm's length. Not exactly. I understand that some of it is probably the old-fashioned way you were raised."

Oh, this just kept getting better and better. "Is that right?" she murmured. "Let me take a wild guess here. You consider me old-fashioned because I haven't jumped in the sack with you like every other woman you've dated."

"Again, being blunt here. Yes. The rest of the world has moved forward, Gia, but the Dantes are still living in a different century, with all the rules, social mores and restrictions that entails. As you know, I was educated at Oxford and enjoy a very sophisticated lifestyle. My entire family actually lives in the twenty-first century."

"Unlike mine." She didn't give him time to respond, instead smiling sweetly. "And for some reason you think a trip to New York will leapfrog me into the current century?"

He countered her smile with a warm, sensuous one of his own. "Hoping, sweetheart. Seriously hoping. Your family is protective. I get that. But still… You're a grown woman, Gia, with emphasis on the *woman*. Why shouldn't you live your life the way you see fit instead of by a set of antiquated rules?"

"Did it ever occur to you that I'm fully aware that I'm a grown woman and that, rather than caving to the old-fashioned dictates of my family, I've deliberately chosen to live by some of those antiquated rules you regard with such disdain?"

He released a sigh. "You're forcing me to spoil the surprise I have planned." He shot her a swift, smoldering look before lifting her left hand and kissing it, his thumb stroking across her bare ring finger. "A surprise that will give everyone cause for celebration and allow your family to turn a blind eye to our little romantic escapade. What do you say to that, sweetheart?"

Gianna's breath caught. Okay, it didn't take a mental genius to add up those clues. He planned to propose. She chose her response with care. "There's nothing I can say, is there? I mean, it's still a future surprise, not an actual proposition." She hesitated. "Is it?"

"Not yet. But I'm hoping to hear a loud, excited 'Yes, David, I will' in the very near future."

Gianna bit down on her lower lip. Gently disengaging their hands, she glanced out the passenger window at Dantes' corporate offices while she fought for control. Why now? Why tonight of all nights? She strongly suspected Constantine would be at the gala. In fact, knowing her family, she could pretty much guarantee it. How could she possibly consider starting an affair, let alone an engagement, with another man while he stood in the wings watching with that fierce, predatory hunger?

Gianna shivered at the thought. She could pretty much guarantee that if she and Constantine had been dating for three months their relationship would have been consummated long ago, whether they'd planned to wait or not. They wouldn't have been able to help themselves. No doubt, he'd have hustled her to the altar at the earliest moment, considering his family was as "old-fashioned," not to mention "antiquated," as hers.

She spared David a brief glance. She always knew this moment would come, when David would force her to make a choice between settling for second best or being alone. She hoped she'd have more time. That her feelings for him would change. But they hadn't and she'd have to make a decision about him—and soon.

He pulled into the parking garage beneath Dantes and slipped into the space reserved for VIP guests. Unbuckling both their seat belts, he surprised her by pulling her into his arms. Then he leaned across the console and kissed her, his warm lips wandering across hers. She allowed the embrace, attempted to lose herself in it.

More than anything, she wanted to fall for David. Wanted The Inferno to strike with someone who wanted her as much as he did. Who would put her first in his life instead of picking her up when he found time—an afterthought that he could discard whenever he tired of her. And why, when David kissed her with such hunger were her thoughts consumed by Constantine? She pulled back, pasting a smile on her face.

"Well?" David prompted softly.

She avoided his gaze. "I need some time," she replied.

He stilled, his expression cooling. "Time. Time to decide about New York? Or time to respond to my surprise?"

"I'm a little distracted by the gala," she explained, avoiding a direct answer. "I also need to check my calendar."

He lifted a light brown eyebrow. "Does that mean you're interested in a romantic weekend and all that entails?"

"I'm interested in discussing it," she temporized. She checked her watch and winced when she saw the time. "I'm sorry, David. I need to get inside. Could we table our discussion until later?"

"Table our discussion," he repeated.

Gianna sighed. "Sorry. I didn't mean to sound so businesslike."

"That's fine. I get it."

Without another word he exited the car. Circling the Jag, he opened her door and helped her out. They walked in silence to the elevators, the silence deepening as they shot upward to the appropriate floor.

The instant she stepped into the hallway, she sensed Constantine. He was nearby. Her reaction, primal and fierce, made her think of jungle animals responding to the pheromones of their mates. Part of her wanted to leave David's side and search through the warren of corridors until she found Constantine.

She closed her eyes and took a deep, steadying breath. This had to stop. Now. She couldn't remain on this emotional roller coaster. Pushing emotion aside she focused on logic and practicality. If she caved to desire she'd be lost. She needed to focus on David d'Angelo. But with every step she took, all her senses remained tuned to one man. Consumed by him.

Constantine Romano. The man who'd stolen her heart and soul.

Two

Gianna stepped into the ballroom to discover that most of her family had already arrived. The instant they caught sight of her they descended and swept her off with David following reluctantly in their wake.

She remembered his comment about her family breathing down their necks and couldn't help wondering if he felt like a Dantes' afterthought the same way she felt like Constantine's afterthought. What a mess.

After checking to ensure that all the various details for the gala had been finalized, Gianna joined her family in the reception line while David helped himself to a flute of champagne and wandered among the various displays, attempting with only limited success to conceal his boredom.

"He is the only man I know who can look at the most beautiful jewelry in the world with all the excitement of someone tasting sour milk," Gianna's brother Rafe growled in her ear. "Make him stop before he sends all of our guests fleeing into the night."

"How do you suggest I do that?"

"Your date. Your problem. But you'd better hurry up or I'll have to go over there and give him an attitude adjustment."

"Are all of you this polite to David when I'm not around?" she asked suspiciously.

Her eldest brother, Luc, joined them, followed by Draco. They started in as though they'd rehearsed their remarks, which possibly they had. "We don't like him," Draco announced, folding his arms across his chest. "And he doesn't like any of us."

"He's preoccupied with money. Granted, he *is* a banker."

"But it's all about the bottom line with him."

"He has no poetry in his soul. He's cold-blooded. We don't want our baby sister married to someone so passionless."

Gianna held up her hands. "Wait a minute. Just wait a minute. You've all been doing the big-brother thing with him, haven't you?" She eyed one after the other of her older siblings, none of whom had the grace to look the least shamefaced. She groaned. "Oh, Lord. You have."

"He didn't pass the test," Rafe explained helpfully. "He refused to attend a Giants game with me. *Box* seats."

Luc nodded in agreement. "Failed miserably. He doesn't even *play* basketball. I don't think he likes to sweat."

"He's a jerk," Draco offered with a toothy grin that would have done a dragon proud. "He turned down a case of Primo's homemade beer. Sneered at it. I've never seen our grandfather so ticked off."

"I would kill for a case of Primo's beer." A new voice dropped into the conversation. A painfully familiar voice. One which had haunted her thoughts and memories for nineteen impossible months. "What a foolish man to turn it down. Who are we talking about? Is this fool a friend of yours, Gianna?"

She spun around to face Constantine, her eyes widening at the sight of him. He was absolutely devastating in his tux, filling it out even better than David. Everything feminine within her responded to him. "What are you doing here, Constantine?" she demanded in a ragged undertone.

"What do you think?" His black gaze fastened on her as though she were the only one present. "I've come to claim what's mine."

From the corner of her eye, she saw David approach. Not that it mattered to Constantine, if he even noticed. Instead, with her date and relatives looking on, he captured her chin in his hand and tilted her face up to his.

And then he consumed her.

Gianna didn't attempt to evade Constantine's kiss, regardless of who was watching. His lips took possession of hers and ignited a flame she'd never experienced with any other man. Definitely not with David. For a brief moment she forgot all those witnessing the potent embrace. Forgot the time, the day, even her own name. All that remained was the strength of Constantine's hold, the heat of his body and that incredible mouth that moved on hers with such possessiveness.

He said so much with that single kiss. He spoke of longing, of their endless parting. Of hunger and intense pleasure. But most of all he spoke of the simple, yet undeniable fact that the two of them belonged together. There was a certainty to his kiss, a confidence in the way he took her mouth. A rightness. He knew her and what she wanted. And he gave it to her.

Any thought of resistance faded. Why would she resist when she wanted this more than she wanted air to breathe? Everything about him drew an elemental response from her.

His crisp, unique scent. The hard, undeniable maleness of his body locked against hers. The molten burn of his touch. Just a single touch and The Inferno went wild, shaking her to the very depths of her being. Even the beat of his heart resonated with her own.

And all the while, the explosive desire that heated their embrace sizzled with an intoxicating joy that they were together once again. She could practically feel his certainty grow with every second that passed, a fierce determination that formed the foundation of his character. It told her that he would have her for his own regardless of what obstacles he faced—including David.

It didn't matter that Constantine came from Italian aristocracy or that he'd been educated in the finest schools or that the Romanos were renowned for their civility and propriety. When stripped of all his social refinement, the man who held her remained a pirate at heart, intent on taking what he considered his. Intent on taking her.

She shivered within his hold, teetering on the brink of surrender. It wasn't until David dropped a hand on her shoulder and literally ripped her from Constantine's arms that she realized where she was—and in whose arms.

Heat burned in Gianna's cheeks and she took another hasty step backward, struggling to regain her composure. How could she have kissed Constantine like that in public, with her entire family looking on, not to mention the A-list roster of clients she'd personally invited to the gala? What must they all be thinking? She spared David a brief glance and cringed at the blatant outrage darkening his expression. No question what *he* thought.

Snatching a deep breath, she fell back on the sort of courtesy she had been taught since the moment she could first form coherent sentences. "David, this is Constantine Romano. He's…well…he's a member of the family. Sort of."

She spared Constantine a swift glance, startled by the flash of recognition when he first looked at David, fury following swiftly. That's right. They had a passing acquaintance. By the looks of things, maybe a passing enmity would better describe it. Tension thickened the air between the two men. "Constantine?" she asked hesitantly.

"I am not a member of the family," he contradicted in a hard voice, adding, "Yet. And David and I have met."

David smiled with a cold, cutting amusement that stole every ounce of charm from his expression. "Romano." He flicked a speck of lint from the cuff of his snowy dress shirt, making her wonder if he'd like to flick Constantine out of his way with a similar disdain. "As usual your timing leaves something to be desired."

Constantine took a step in his direction and to her alarm, her brothers packed in behind him. "What you mean is…as usual, I've arrived just in time." He spoke to Gianna without taking his gaze off David. "Is this him?" he demanded. "Is d'Angelo the bastard you told me about?"

How in the world did she answer that? She couldn't remember ever feeling so uncomfortable before. "He's the man I mentioned to you, yes," she confessed. "We've been dating for the past couple of months."

"You don't owe Romano an explanation," David said. "He's not a factor in your life, any more than he's a member of your family."

"To the contrary. Gianna and I are discussing ways we might change that. In the very near future I intend to be a permanent fixture in her life."

David froze and his intense blue eyes narrowed. Sharpened. "What the hell do you mean by that?"

Constantine smiled, a dangerous, predatory baring of his teeth. "I mean just what you think I mean. I've moved to

San Francisco with the express intention of asking Gianna to do me the honor of becoming my wife."

Conversation exploded around them. "Oh, God," Gianna murmured, swaying in place.

As though from a great distance she could hear the excitement and approval of her family, the congratulations that made it clear that the Dantes were firmly aligned in Constantine's corner of this hideous triangle. She spun to face an infuriated David.

He gathered up his self-control and forced out a smile. She couldn't begin to imagine how much effort it took. "You're delusional, Romano. Gia and I already have an understanding, one that will be cemented on our upcoming trip to New York City. A private suite at the Ritz. Candlelight and roses." He gestured carelessly toward one of the display cases. "Is Sev the one I should see in order to purchase a Dantes' engagement ring? I'm assuming Tiffany's or Cartier is out of the question. A shame really."

Dead silence followed David's comment. She could feel the waves of fury pouring off Constantine, which was no doubt the point. And after the crack about Tiffany's and Cartier, her family didn't appear any calmer. How could David be so foolish? It was so unlike him. Granted, he hadn't formed the sort of tight relationship with her brothers she'd hoped he would, but he'd never been deliberately rude. In fact, he'd always been polite, intent on making a good impression, even if it lacked a certain warmth.

Time to act, Gianna realized, and fast. The first item on her agenda was to remove David from the line of fire before someone decked him. Then they'd have a talk. A *long* talk. She needed to decide once and for all whether there was any possibility of a future for her with David. If not, the only honorable option was to end things between them.

"If you'll excuse us, my date and I have a few important matters to discuss," Gianna announced.

David grinned in triumph and dropped an arm around her shoulders, tugging her into his arms. For a split second she thought matters might turn physical. Maybe they would have if David's impromptu embrace hadn't placed her squarely between the warring factions. An accident, she was certain. Her oldest brother, Luc, grabbed Constantine's shoulder in one hand and Rafe's in the other, actively restraining the two men.

"Later," she heard him murmur. "This isn't the proper time or place."

Clearly David had no intention of waiting for the proper time or place. "Yes, boys, heel" came his parting shot before he swept her away.

"What is going on?" she demanded in an undertone.

His congenial mask faded. "I planned to ask you the precise same questions."

"Answer mine, first. What's between you and Constantine?"

"Old history. Nothing to do with us. Come." He gestured toward the terrace off the ballroom. "Let's find somewhere private to talk."

Though it was midsummer, a cool haze embraced their surroundings, creating a pale, misty curtain. The sprawl of the city glittered softly through the veil, muffling sight, sound and light. It was almost as though they were cut off from the rest of the world, trapped within an oasis of fog. Tables dotted the terrace, situated in cozy, shadow-draped alcoves. David selected the most private.

"Why don't you sit here for a moment while I get us both a drink."

She wasn't going to let him off the hook. "Then you'll explain?"

"Absolutely. Just as you will."

She heard the clipped warning in his voice and winced. She didn't look forward to that part of the conversation at all. She used her time alone to consider how to describe her relationship to Constantine, not to mention that kiss. It would be lovely if she could get away with a short: "It's none of your business." But she knew David better than that.

Before she could come up with a firm plan, he returned with a flute of champagne for her and a Campari for himself. He even offered a congenial smile. After his earlier anger, his sudden equanimity surprised her. She took a sip of champagne and wrinkled her nose at the aftertaste. What in the world…? She'd had this wine before and never experienced the faintly bitter finish she did on this occasion.

He raised his highball glass. "To us."

Aware that David was waiting for a response, she quickly switched gears and tipped her flute in his direction. "To us," she hastened to repeat, gently tapping her glass against his and took another tongue-curdling sip of her wine. As much as she preferred to avoid the coming confrontation, she knew she couldn't. But maybe she could delay her own explanation by taking the offensive. "What's going on, David?"

"You tell me." He eyed her over the rim of his glass. Though he'd banked his anger, she could sense it smoldering just beneath the surface. "That wasn't exactly a familial kiss you exchanged with Romano."

"We're old friends."

"*Intimate* old friends?"

She couldn't discern his expression in the darkness of the terrace, but his tone didn't require the bright light of day to decipher. He was flat-out furious. She took her time responding, sipping her champagne, then wished she hadn't bothered. She chose her words with care. "We dated," she admitted. "Very, very briefly."

"You slept with him."

Anger rippled through her and she set her flute on the table, the crystal singing against the wrought iron. "That's none of your business."

She thought he'd argue the point. He must have reconsidered, because he shrugged. "You're right. It isn't," he conceded. He lifted her glass and handed it to her again, in what was clearly meant to be a peace offering. "I was jealous. Considering that kiss you and Romano exchanged, is it surprising?"

"I guess not."

She accepted the glass. This time when she sipped, she attempted to analyze what was off about the wine. It wasn't flat or sour. The carbonation remained strong and crisp, the flavor light and fruity with a hint of yeast. And yet, the bitterness persisted. She made a mental note to check with the caterer. For now, she'd let the problem go and give her full attention to David.

"So, is it over between you and Romano?" David pressed.

"I'm not sure," she admitted honestly.

It certainly hadn't felt over, not after that kiss. Her palm itched and she curled her fingers inward, wishing she could ignore the sensation. How many Dantes had described that exact same reaction and attributed it to the connection formed when they'd first touched their soul mate? Every last one of them. She closed her eyes. Since Constantine's return, the itching had grown progressively more noticeable. She could sit here with David and deny it until dawn broke across the horizon, but it wouldn't change the facts.

She and Constantine were connected in a way she and David weren't…and quite possibly never would be, no matter how hard she'd tried to ignite that connection.

"Finish your drink, Gia, and then let's go."

The clipped order caught her off guard. Had he seen the regret on her face? "Go? Go, where?"

"For a drive. We need to talk and I'd rather not do it here where Dantes or Romano could burst in on us at any moment." She caught the gleam of his smile in the darkness. "Besides, it will give everyone time to cool off. Don't you think that's the smartest choice?"

Gianna weighed her options. If they stayed, chances were excellent that her family would appear within the next ten minutes with some excuse or another, no doubt one related to business. She toyed with her wineglass and grimaced. Particularly if they tasted the champagne. She didn't have a single doubt that Constantine would head the parade of invaders. He wouldn't be able to help himself. She closed her eyes, an unexpected wave of exhaustion settling over her. She couldn't deal with any of that tonight, she really couldn't.

"Finish your champagne and let's go," David prompted again.

"Okay." But instead of drinking, she set it aside. She could tell her actions didn't please him and wasn't quite certain if he objected to her contrariness or the fact that he'd gone to the trouble of bringing her a drink she hadn't bothered to finish. She touched his hand to distract him. "But then you'll explain about you and Constantine and whatever this old history is between you, right? His sister, Ariana, is married to my cousin Lazz, remember? And I flat-out adore her. I don't want your disagreement with Constantine to interfere with my relationship with her."

"Of course not." He stood and held out his hand. "Why don't we slip out the back way?"

"If it'll avoid a confrontation, I'm all for it," Gianna agreed.

* * *

"Why didn't you tell me they were dating?" Constantine demanded of Gianna's brothers.

Luc shrugged. "Didn't know it had anything to do with you."

Draco frowned. "And just out of curiosity, why does it have anything to do with you?"

Time to make one thing crystal clear to all the Dantes. Constantine folded his arms across his chest and eyed them one by one. "From now on everything about Gianna has to do with me," he stated.

"Wait a minute, wait a minute." Rafe held up his hands. "I know you two met at Lazz's wedding. But when the hell did it go from how-do-you-do to she's-mine-let's-kill-the-competition? Not that I mind, you understand. I'd just like you to fill in a few of the blanks."

How could they even ask that question? They knew how The Inferno worked. They must know what Gianna had chosen to do to him. "It went from one to the other as soon as we shook hands."

Luc's brows shot upward. "The Inferno?"

"She Infernoed you?" Rafe burst out laughing. "Way to go, little sister."

"This is not a laughing matter." Constantine could hear his accent deepening and fought for control. "It might have been polite to ask before she…Infernoed me."

Draco gave him a sympathetic slap on the back. "Yeah, sorry about that. Doesn't really work that way, I'm afraid."

Constantine's eyes narrowed. "When we have more time, perhaps you would be so kind as to explain exactly how it does work."

"Hell, if any of us knew that we wouldn't all be standing here with a ball and chain manacled to our ankles," Rafe said cheerfully. He shot out his hand and captured his wife's wrist, reeling her in. "Isn't that right, my sweet little chain?"

"You just said that because you knew I was standing there, didn't you?" Larkin demanded crossly.

"If you can't handle the truth, don't eavesdrop." Her mouth opened to give him a piece of her mind and he took immediate advantage. They both reemerged a moment later, a bit bewitched and bewildered. He cupped his wife's face and gazed down at her with unmistakable adoration. "Just so you know, I've never been more grateful for that chain or the fact that it goes both ways…and I always will."

A short time later, Gianna found herself in David's car, pulling out of the Dantes' garage. He gave the Jaguar its head, the powerful car eating up the hills of the city a little faster than she'd have liked. He was so different from Constantine. It was almost as though David had something to prove. As though he were trying to show her that he was the better man. Instead of being impressed, she found his actions vaguely sad.

She yawned. "Where are we going?"

"Nowhere in particular. I just thought we'd take a drive out of the city, then park and talk."

He sped through a yellow light and she touched his arm. For some reason it took serious effort, almost as though her limbs had turned to lead. Preparing for the gala must have worn her out more than she realized. "Pull over for just a minute."

"Wait until we're out of the city."

"No, seriously. Pull over. I want you to do something for me."

He spared her a brief, impatient look, then braked a little harder than necessary and rolled to a stop in a red zone beside a fire hydrant. "Okay, I've pulled over. Now what?"

"Would you kiss me?"

A streetlight cut across his face, giving the illusion that his pale eyes were translucent. She could still read his reaction—a mixed one. Part of him wanted her with a deep, primal hunger that he didn't bother to disguise. Another part, one she suspected he would have hidden from her if he could, hesitated. She knew why. He'd guessed she wanted to compare his kiss to the one Constantine had given her. And he'd be right.

The time for pretense was over. She needed to know the truth, once and for all. Either she had serious feelings for David or she didn't. For the past three months she'd thrown herself into the relationship, hoping against hope that desire would flare to life. That The Inferno would strike with him, the way it had with Constantine. She knew for a fact that could happen. Even so, she couldn't create a fire without combustible materials. At the very least she should feel as if she'd struck a match when they kissed. Generated a hint of smoke. Created a flicker or two of flame. Something. If not, the only honorable course was to end things between them.

David took his time. Reaching for her, he drew her as close as possible given the console between them. He cupped her face and leaned in, taking her mouth slowly, then more passionately. His breathing grew ragged as the moments slipped by and his fingers thrust into her hair so he could control and deepen the kiss.

It took every ounce of self-possession to keep from jerking free of his hold. His touch felt wrong. Wrong on every conceivable level. No matter how hard she attempted to fight it, there was only one man for her. And he wasn't the one kissing her.

Even so, she didn't fight him or pull back, despite the muffled instinct urging her to do just that. For some reason it felt as though she'd left her brain on the terrace at Dantes, trapped within that dense summer fog. More than anything she wished she could curl up and go to sleep. Maybe a drive wasn't the best option.

It wasn't until he groped for the fastening of the halter top of her gown that she stirred. "No, David." He pulled back, a protest blazing across his face. Before he could say anything, her cell phone rang, loud and strident within the confines of the car. It cut through the drag of exhaustion, giving her a moment of clarity. "I need to get that."

"No, you don't," he argued. "For once in your life, ignore your family."

"I'm a Dante, David," she explained gently. "You know it doesn't work that way. They'll worry if I don't answer."

She took the call, but instead of one of her brothers as she expected, it was Constantine who spoke. "Where are you, *piccola?*" he asked.

"With David. We're going for a drive."

A brief silence, then, "Tell him to take you straight home."

"Is that an order?"

"There's something you should know about David, Gianna. It's important. I wouldn't ask if it weren't."

She might have argued, but with David sitting there listening to every word, she decided to choose prudence for once in her life. "I'll call you later when it's more convenient."

"I'm leaving Dantes in another few minutes. I'll wait outside your place until I hear from you."

She sighed. "It might be a bit. David and I..." She spared her date a brief glance, not the least surprised by the anger sparking in his gaze. Could he hear Constantine's voice, tell it wasn't one of her brothers who'd called? Or had he guessed what was happening based on her responses? "We need to talk."

"Going to dump him?"

"That's none of your business."

"Everything about you is my business," he responded with devastating simplicity.

She flipped the phone closed and dropped it in her purse. "David—"

"Don't."

She fought through her exhaustion, attempting to find the kindest, gentlest words possible. "David, let's be honest with each other. We've been dating for three months. If we shared something that could have become permanent, we'd have felt it by now."

"We have felt it," he argued. "You can't deny you feel something for me. You've just allowed Romano to confuse you. Give me a chance, Gia. Give *us* a chance."

It was truth time. She would never want this man. Not the way a woman should want the man who hoped to share her bed. No matter how hard she tried, no matter how she attempted to lose herself in David's embrace, some part of her remained remote and untouched. That secret part of herself flinched from allowing any other man to hold her. Touch her. Kiss her. Only one man had that right. She closed her eyes, caving to the inevitable. There wouldn't be a private weekend in New York. Or a romantic suite at the Ritz, not to mention an engagement.

Nor would she ever share David's bed.

"I have given us a chance," she told him as compassionately as she could manage. She fought back another yawn. The fog returned, relentless, rolling toward her at breakneck speed. "It's not working."

"I'll make it work." He turned a knob on the console

which put the Jag in gear and fishtailed away from the curb. "Lean back and close your eyes, Gia. We'll be there before you know it."

She shook her head, but it didn't help. The fog descended, consuming her, and she tumbled into its cold gray embrace. "What's wrong with me?" she murmured.

"Put your seat back and go to sleep. When you wake it'll all be over."

What would be over? But it took too much effort to ask the question. And she slept.

Three

"She's not at her house and she's not answering her cell." Constantine paced up and down the sidewalk for the umpteenth time. After twenty endless minutes, he knew every crack and stain by heart. "That can only mean one thing. D'Angelo has her. There's no other possibility."

Luc sighed. "He doesn't *have* her. They're simply out together. I hate to say this, Constantine, but they've been dating for a couple of months. She's a grown woman. If she isn't answering her cell it's because she doesn't want to talk to you. I'm sure she'll be in touch in the morning."

"No," Constantine snarled into his cell phone. Every instinct he possessed screamed in protest. He had to find her. *Now.* "If we wait until morning, it will be too late. He knows I am on to him. He'll have to move tonight if he has any hope of keeping her from me."

"What the bloody hell are you talking about?" Luc snapped.

Constantine forced himself to explain in a calm, crisp manner that didn't sound like *he* was the deranged one, rather than d'Angelo. "D'Angelo has drugged at least one other woman in the past in order to take advantage of her. *Attempted* to take advantage of her. I stopped him in time."

"Dear God. *That's* what he meant about your timing leaving something to be desired?"

"Yes." Constantine checked his watch, also for the umpteenth time. "If d'Angelo wishes to do this to Gianna…if he wishes to drug her and take advantage of her, where would he take her?"

There was a brief silence and Constantine could practically hear Luc mentally sorting through the possibilities. "He's renting a suite at one of the hotels here in the city while he waits for escrow to close on the mansion he's purchased. I don't remember which hotel, though I could probably find out. One of the pricier ones, I'm sure."

Constantine considered for a moment, then shook his head. "No, he wouldn't take her to his hotel. Too many witnesses. It would be someplace private."

"Let me check around." Sick tension bled across the airwaves. "I'll get back to you."

"Make it fast," Constantine advised. "The clock is ticking."

"Romano—" Fear ripped apart Luc's voice.

"Remain calm. I'll find her. And I'll be in time."

For the sake of his sanity, he didn't have any choice.

Gianna stirred, slowly surfacing, vaguely aware that the Jaguar was slowing. The wipers were on, swishing softly while rain pelted against the windshield. Were they home? She must have fallen asleep during the brief drive, she realized groggily. How strange. Her head lolled toward the window and she squinted at the darkness that consumed the car. No, not home, she realized. They weren't even in the city.

"David?" she murmured sleepily.

"Almost there. I hadn't planned to make this trip tonight, so I need to stop for gas. Then it's not much farther."

"Where are we?"

"A little north of Calistoga."

The information filtered through with sludgelike speed. When it did, the confusion clouding her mind began to clear. *Calistoga?* It took her a moment to place it. When she did, her breath caught. That was a solid hour outside of the city at the north end of the Napa Valley. Why in the world would he have driven so far? It didn't make sense. "I don't understand. What are we doing in Calistoga?"

He spared her a brief, impatient look. "You should have finished your champagne. You were supposed to sleep until we reached the lodge."

Once again it took time to sort through his comment, but little by little she could feel the sluggishness fading away. She didn't understand the wine comment and focused instead on his second statement. Lodge? What lodge? "I'm not going to any lodge with you. I want you to take me home."

"I'll be happy to." He paused a beat. "Tomorrow."

She shook her head in protest, shocked by the weight of it. Why was it so heavy? She could barely hold it up. "Something's wrong with me," she said. "I feel so odd."

"You're just tired. Put your seat back and go to sleep."

He'd said that to her before. This time it wasn't a request, but an order, so firmly delivered, she almost didn't resist. More than anything she wanted to obey him and surrender to the darkness just waiting to consume her once again. The champagne. He'd said something about the champagne.

"You drugged me." She didn't pose it as a question.

Instead of protesting, he grinned like a schoolboy caught with his hand in the cookie jar. "Maybe just a little."

Fear, sudden and abrupt, coursed through her system burning through the remaining mists blanketing her thoughts. He'd drugged her. Dear God, he'd actually drugged her. She attempted to moisten her lips but found it impossible. Her mouth and throat had gone bone-dry.

"Why?" she managed to ask. "Why would you do that to me?"

He shrugged, taut muscles rippling beneath the impressive expanse of his dress shirt. He must have removed his tux jacket at some point while she slept. She shuddered. What else had happened while she'd been unconscious?

"Because I want you," he admitted, as though that were explanation enough.

And maybe it was, for him. She'd always been aware that he possessed an overdeveloped sense of entitlement. More than once she'd heard him excuse the occasional excessive indulgence with the excuse, "But I deserve…" Whether a suite at the Ritz-Carlton or a third Rolex or a fully loaded Jaguar, David always felt entitled to the best. Apparently he'd now decided that he "deserved" her. Anger ripped through her, combating the drugs, as well as her fear. Well, not if she could help it.

"It doesn't bother you that drugging and kidnapping me was the only way you could achieve your ends?" she asked. Maybe if she kept him talking, it would give her time to think…and plan a way out of this.

"Drugging you wasn't the only way, just the most expeditious."

He took his eyes off the road long enough to frown in her direction. It occurred to her that if she had any hope of escaping her present predicament, she'd be wise to pretend the drugs had a stronger hold on her than they did. Otherwise, he might decide to administer a little more and she'd never get away. She closed her eyes with a soft sigh and allowed her head to roll to one side.

"So sleepy," she murmured.

He trailed the back of his hand along the curve of her cheek and it took every ounce of self-control to keep from flinching. "Trust me. By morning you'll wonder why you held me off for so long. And by tomorrow afternoon…"

"By tomorrow afternoon…?" She deliberately yawned out the question.

"We'll be engaged."

She lifted a hand to her forehead. "I…I don't understand."

"Once I explain what happened to your grandfather, abashed and contrite that we allowed passion to overcome Dante propriety, your family will demand I do the honorable thing and marry you. In fact, I'll insist it's the only reasonable solution."

She stiffened in outrage. What the hell did he know about honor? She almost asked the question, keeping her mouth shut at the last instant. Being a *chiacchierona* as her family affectionately called her—a chatterbox—wouldn't help in her current situation. Restraint and discretion would.

"I seem to remember hearing that Luc and Téa found themselves in a similar predicament—caught in the act— and Primo insisted they marry immediately," David continued with a pensive air. "I'm sure he'll be even more insistent with his only granddaughter, if only to uphold the family honor."

"And if I tell my grandfather you drugged me?" She fought to keep the sharpness from her voice and ask the question in a vague, confused manner.

He chuckled. "You won't remember that, any more tha̶n you'll remember this conversation."

He pulled into a gas station, the only spot of brightnes̶s along the remote stretch of road. Darkness poured fro̶m the interior of the cement block storefront. No help there̶. Nor from the closed and padlocked service bay doors. Bu̶t the pumps were lit and available for credit card purchases̶. Maybe someone else would stop for gas. Someone wh̶o could help her.

He turned in the leather seat to face her. "Before you fa̶l̶l̶ back asleep, I have one final question for you."

"Can't. Too tired."

"Ah, ah, ah," he scolded, giving her a little shake. "Yo̶u can sleep after you answer my question."

She made a feeble gesture for him to continue befor̶e allowing her hand to flop back onto her lap. "What?" Sh̶e deliberately slurred the word.

"Where's Brimstone?"

She blinked, staring at him blankly, unable to make sens̶e of the words. And not because of the drugs. "What?"

"The Dante fire diamond, Brimstone. Where is it?" h̶e asked urgently. "My sources tell me it disappeared. Wha̶t happened to it?"

"I don't know what you're talking about."

He swore in Italian. "Don't give me that. It's practicall̶y a Dante legend. My father told me all about it and he got i̶t straight from Vittorio Romano."

Vittorio. Constantine's father. "I…I don't know anythin̶g about it."

"It was supposed to go to the Romanos after you̶r cousin and Ariana married. But it never did." He pause̶d̶, speaking more to himself than to her. "Unless that bastar̶d̶, Constantine, financed Romano Restoration with it. I can̶'t imagine any other way he could have done it in so short̶ time. Not with my father blocking his every attempt to get a loan."

She forced out a yawn. "I'm so tired…I don't understand a word you're saying."

He took a moment to think it through. "If Romano has the diamond, he wouldn't be here, sniffing after you. And despite what my sources say, you don't just lose a fire diamond as valuable as Brimstone. Which means…" His focus returned to her. "Does your family still have the diamond? Is that why Romano's here? That's it, isn't it? He's hoping to romance it out from under you by marrying into the family."

"Never heard of Brimstone," she mumbled.

And she hadn't. But she sure as hell intended to ask about it the minute she got herself out of her current predicament. She shuddered. Assuming she could. Please, God, let someone come.

His gaze pinned her in place, sharp and ruthless. "Fine. Pretend you don't know. It won't change a thing. Once I've married into the family, it won't matter, anyway."

"'Kay." She closed her eyes and slumped in her seat.

"Gia?"

She didn't so much as twitch.

"Gianna!"

She kept her breathing slow and deep. She never realized how much effort it took to feign sleep when her heart galloped like a racehorse and panic threatened to consume her. She must have convinced David, though. She heard him push a button near the steering wheel which she gathered released the gas tank cover, then he opened the car door and exited. Peeking from beneath her lashes, she held her breath while he circled to stand at the rear of the car with his back to her and removed his wallet from his pocket, extracting a credit card.

She wouldn't get a better opportunity. She'd watched him start the Jag any number of times. It didn't require a key. She simply had to apply the brakes, then push the "start" button on the console between the two seats. Once the engine fired, a knob popped up which controlled the gear settings. After that, matters might get a bit more dicey.

The instant David inserted his credit card in the gas pump, she moved, slinging her legs over the center console and sliding into the driver's seat. She jammed the door release lever with her elbow, locking all the doors. Next she hit the brake with both feet and slapped the start/stop button on the console. The Jag purred to life. Just as she'd seen countless times before, the gear knob released.

Behind her, she heard David shout. Not that she listened. She turned the button from P for Park to D for Drive. Now for the tricky part. To drive a car for the second time in her entire life. Taking a deep breath, she hit the gas.

The Jag responded with a throaty roar of enthusiasm and leaped forward, careening across the cement lot toward the road. She fought to contain the power, jerking the wheel one way and then the other. The Jag responded to every movement—and then some. She attempted to compensate for her oversteer, overcorrected instead, and the back of the vehicle fishtailed, the tires screaming at her mistreatment.

Slow down, slow down!

But for some reason she couldn't peel her foot off the accelerator. She was too desperate to escape to let up. Just before she reached the road the right side of the car hit a curb, sending it spinning. It made a half dozen 360s across the two-lane road before clipping a tree with its rear end. Metal shrieked, airbags exploded around her. Then silence descended.

The Jag had come to rest facing the gas station. She'd

made her escape, all right. She'd gotten a solid two hundred yards down the road. For a split second, she and David stared at each other. Then with a shout of fury, he charged in her direction.

Gianna fought for breath. This was not going to end well.

"Calistoga?" Constantine punched the name into his GPS. "Where the hell is Calistoga?"

"This I do not know," Vittorio Romano responded. The connection faded for a brief moment then kicked in again. "The business associate mentioned a fancy lodge that the d'Angelo boy owns near this Calistoga. He uses it to entertain clients."

For once, the nine-hour time difference between Italy and California had worked to Constantine's advantage. It might be after midnight for him, but it was bright and early in the morning at the Romano palazzo. "A suite at the Ritz. A mansion. A Jag. Now a lodge. I have to tell you, Babbo. All these years we've been doing something wrong."

"Something right," his father corrected. "I have been hearing rumors about the d'Angelos and their banking practices. Creative accounting is the term being thrown about. Soon, all of Firenze will be talking. It won't be long before they are talking in San Francisco, too."

"Too bad the rumors couldn't have hit the States a couple of months ago," Constantine muttered. He checked the GPS. "Okay, I've found Calistoga. Do you have an address?"

"No. But I am still waiting for information from another source."

"Call me as soon as you hear anything."

Constantine didn't waste any more time. Once more the late hour worked to his advantage and he drove onto the Golden Gate Bridge in record time. If he broke every speed

record out there, he could make it to Calistoga in under an
hour. That would still put him a solid thirty minutes behind
d'Angelo. Maybe longer.

His hands tightened on the steering wheel. If he thought
about what was happening to her, what d'Angelo might be
doing right now, he'd go insane. *Focus.* First, he'd focus on
getting to Calistoga as quickly as possible. Then he'd focus
on finding Gianna. But the instant he found her and ensured
her safety... David d'Angelo would regret ever touching his
woman. Or any other woman, for that matter. He planned
to see to that.

Personally.

Move, move, *move!*

Gianna thrust open the door and erupted from the Jag.
At the last instant she remembered her cell phone. Flinging
herself across the driver's seat, she batted the deflated
airbags out of her way and snagged her beaded handbag
from the passenger side floor. Sparing a swift glance in
David's direction—heaven protect her, he was close—she
darted into the forest along the side of the road.

Rain pelted her. It soaked her dress, causing it to cling to
her legs, making running awkward. Worse, bushes grabbed
at her ankles, threatening to trip her up. But it was her
mile-high heels sinking into the boggy earth that ultimately
did her in. She went down, the wet, needle-strewn ground
absorbing the impact of her fall and cushioning her rolling
descent into a shallow depression. A small, shocked cry
escaped before she could suppress it. She could only hope
the rain muffled the sound.

As it turned out the fall saved her from discovery. David
crashed through the underbrush practically on her heels.
She heard him standing directly above her, his breathing
harsh and ragged from the exertion of chasing after her. He

would have seen her if she weren't enveloped by the heavy, protective darkness of the depression.

"Gia! Don't be an idiot," he shouted. For the first time since she'd known him, his Italian accent came through loud and clear. It was nowhere near as smooth and lyrical as Constantine's, but coarse and discordant. "Come out. This is all some hideous mistake."

Gianna didn't so much as breathe. Sure thing. She'd come on out and he could explain the mistake while he…how had he put it? The words came back to her through the lingering effect of the drug he'd poisoned her with. While he allowed passion to overcome Dante propriety. Yeah, right. Not a chance in hell. She closed her eyes like a child hiding from the boogeyman. If she couldn't see him, he couldn't see her.

He thrashed back toward the Jag and swore. "Look what you did to my car." He called her a name in Italian, one she hadn't heard before. Probably best she didn't know what it meant. "Do you have any idea how much it'll cost me to have this fixed?"

Slowly she stood and kicked off her heels, deciding that going barefoot, no matter how difficult, made more sense than risking a twisted ankle or broken leg. If that happened, she'd be at David's mercy. She squinted through the rain. In the darkness, the woods appeared impenetrable.

She was wet and cold, with bracken clinging to her skin, hair and clothes. She could only hope that the dirt helped camouflage her. She held her arms out in front of her so she wouldn't run blindly into a tree and stepped gingerly across the forest carpet. Rocks and sticks littered the area and she winced at the scrape and poke. Little by little, she slipped deeper into the woods.

She didn't want to stray so far from the road that she couldn't find her way back. But she also didn't dare stay close enough that David might find her. In the distance, she heard the Jag start and hoped she hadn't damaged it so badly he couldn't leave.

Please, leave!

Lights flickered across the trees and then stopped, shining directly toward her. She instantly dropped to a crouch behind a huge, thick evergreen, possibly a redwood. The car door popped opened and slammed closed, and David's shadow flashed across the path of the headlights. He hurried into the woods once again, using the high beams to guide him.

Gianna hugged the tree, shivering, its rough bark cutting into her exposed skin. Until that moment she hadn't realized how cold she was. Maybe fear or adrenaline had kept her from feeling anything else. No doubt reaction was setting in. She didn't dare move, knowing he'd find her instantly if she did. All the while he came closer, making a beeline in her direction. Could he see her? Sense her? Had he found the trail she'd left through the brush? Unable to help herself, she rocked back and forth, a whimper of terror building in her throat. *Please let him give up and drive away,* she prayed. *Please.*

Her prayers were answered a moment later. In the distance she heard the sound of an approaching vehicle, something large and heavy. A truck? With the damaged Jag skewed across the road so it could face the woods, chances were excellent the driver would stop to help.

David froze at the sound, not more than a dozen feet away. He must have come to the same conclusion she had about the approaching vehicle because he swore violently. "Fine. Freeze to death for all I care, you crazy bitch," he shouted. She heard him retreat at a swift clip as the truck lumbered closer. "But you're paying for the damage you did to my car, you hear me?"

He really was insane. She couldn't think of any other explanation for such irrational behavior. She heard the car door slam and he gunned the engine repeatedly before taking off. Something metallic banged and rattled along behind the Jag. Maybe the rear bumper or the muffler. It must have come loose because she heard it bounce along the road before clattering onto the shoulder as David roared away. An instant later, the truck flashed by and disappeared. No help from that direction.

She waited for endless moments, straining for any hint that David might have changed his mind and returned. Then she remembered her cell phone. She leaned her forehead against the tree trunk and fought back a hot rush of tears. She'd dropped her purse at some point during her escape, probably when she'd fallen down the incline. Gathering herself up, she dropped to the ground on hands and knees and began to search.

Inch by agonizing inch, minute by bone-freezing minute, she worked her way toward the depression, fanning her hands through the bracken littering the forest floor. More than anything, she wanted to curl into a ball and weep hysterically. She didn't dare. She didn't think she'd last through the night if she lost control now. But she was close, so close to giving up and giving in. Then her hand glanced off the slick beads of her purse.

Shock was setting in, along with a numbing cold. Her fingers shook so hard it took three attempts to open the stubborn clasp of her handbag. Even when she managed that, she could barely hold on to the phone. She didn't have a hope in hell of punching out a number. It took her an instant to realize David must have switched her phone off while she'd been unconscious. It took her full concentration just to get it powered back on. The instant it flared to life, her cell phone gave a soft beep warning that her battery was running low.

No. Oh, no, no, *no!* This was not happening. She literally would not be able to handle it if her phone died now. How many times had she drained the battery because she'd forgotten to plug it in? She suspected that wouldn't happen again—ever. And how ironic that David's turning it off, no doubt to keep any incoming calls from waking her, had preserved the last of the cell's battery power.

She managed to punch Redial with a trembling finger. An instant later Constantine answered.

"Gianna?"

She burst into tears. "Help."

Four

Constantine raced into the service station at full speed and braked the Porsche to a screaming halt beneath one of the lighted gas pump overhangs.

He scanned the area. Nothing. No one.

Gianna's cell had died midway through the call and he could only hope that he'd found the right gas station on the right road. The rain had subsided in the past fifteen minutes, easing off to a fitful mist. But that didn't change the fact that she was out there somewhere in the wet and cold.

He tore open the car door and burst from the vehicle. "Gianna?" he shouted. His voice bounced and echoed off the concrete lot and buildings, an eerie sound in the stillness of the night. "Where are you, *piccola?*"

A movement across the street caught his eye and Gianna exploded from the undergrowth. She took one look at him, and his name escaped in a low, choked whimper. In the next instant, she lifted the drenched skirts of her gown to halfway up her thighs and raced barefoot across the street toward him, splashing haphazardly through the puddles in her path, the back of her dress making wet slapping noises against her bare legs. He froze for a split second, gut-wrenching relief fading in the face of horrified concern.

He barely recognized her. Gone was the elegant woman he'd seen earlier in the evening, replaced by a filthy, bedraggled waif. Debris covered her from head to toe, dirt ground into what little he could see of the torn sweep of her skirt. Scratches gouged the pale skin of her arms and legs. And her feet… He swore silently. Her poor, bare feet. He didn't know how she could walk, let alone run. Maybe the shock kept her from feeling the pain.

He charged toward her, meeting her halfway. She flung herself into his arms and he wrapped her in an unbreakable hold, relieved beyond measure at finding her alive and safe. She burrowed against him, weeping and talking and shuddering so hard he couldn't make out a word she said. Damn it to hell, she was freezing.

He lifted her into his arms and carried her rapidly to the car. "I need to get you warm," he warned. "We have to get you out of these wet clothes."

She was too far gone to process his words. He set her down again and she winced the instant her feet hit the pavement. He silently swore again. D'Angelo would pay for every last scratch on Gianna…and pay dearly. Reaching behind her, he fumbled for the closure of her halter gown. Unable to figure it out, he dealt with it in the simplest, most expeditious way. He ripped it off her.

"Easy, *piccola,* easy," he soothed. "I'm just trying to get you dry and warm."

He stripped her in one swift move, steeling himself against her distress and confusion and weeping protests. Then he yanked off his own shirt and tux jacket and helped her into them before urging her to the passenger side of the car. The instant he had her buckled in, he cranked up the heat.

It took her three tries to speak. "You scared me for a minute there, but I get it now," she murmured in a low, shaky voice. She waved a hand to indicate his shirt and jacket. "The undressing and dressing to warm me up thing, I mean. Thanks."

"Are you okay?" He shook his head at his own stupidity. "Foolish question. I should say, did d'Angelo... Did he hurt you?"

He couldn't use the real word for it. But he could tell from her expression she understood what he meant. She folded her legs against her chest and wrapped her arms around them, hugging herself for warmth no doubt. She splayed blue-tipped fingers in front of the air vent and released a blissful sigh, before answering his question.

"I got away before he could."

He probably shouldn't push. Not now. But he couldn't help himself. "How did you manage it? To escape, I mean? I'm surprised you weren't out cold the entire time." Her head jerked around and unspoken questions filled her gaze in response to his observation. He shrugged. "I know d'Angelo drugged you. He's done it before."

Her eyes widened, went black with shock as she assimilated the information. "I would have been out cold," she confessed after a long moment. Her wet hair curled wildly around a face gone bone-white. "At least, that's what David said. But I didn't finish the champagne. It tasted...off. So, I didn't get a full dose of whatever he'd given me."

Madre di Dio. Luck. It all boiled down to sheer, unadulterated luck. "When did you wake?"

"Right before he stopped for gas. He...he was going to compromise me so that Primo would insist we marry."

Apparently she couldn't use the actual words for what d'Angelo had almost done, any more than Constantine could. It was too soon. The words too vile. The events still so new and raw that they defied full comprehension. "It probably would have worked if I hadn't escaped while he was running his credit card through the gas pump."

It had been close. Unbelievably close. If she'd finished her drink, she wouldn't have woken until far too late. If David hadn't needed gas, he wouldn't have stopped the car until they reached his lodge. If Gianna had been too frightened to keep her wits about her, to think and plan and act on the spur of the moment, she'd never have run when the opportunity had presented itself. Providence had smiled. On both of them.

"What do you say we get out of here?" he asked gently.

She managed a shaky smile. "Yes, please."

He put the car in gear and headed south toward the city at a far more circumspect speed than the trip north. "We should call Luc and let him know you're safe. I'm sure he's going out of his mind with worry."

"My cell is dead."

He fished his out of his pocket and handed it to her. She placed the call and spoke at length to her brother, making light of the experience, describing it as an unfortunate "mis-understanding." When she disconnected the call, Constantine shot her a sharp look, one she avoided.

"Why did you lie to him?"

She released an exhausted sigh. "You know why. If I told Luc what really happened, my brothers would take David apart limb by limb."

"That's going to happen, anyway."

"But—"

"Why the hell are you defending him?" Constantine nearly growled.

Tears threatened. "I'm not defending him. I am *not* defending him," she repeated. It took her a moment to gather herself. "Do you really think that if I went to the police it would help? I have no proof. It'll be my word against his. And the publicity—" Her voice broke and she swiveled to stare out the window. After a moment, she said, "I did wreck his Jag. You have no idea how much pleasure that gives me, knowing I did that much."

Well, hell. "How did you do that?"

"I crashed it into a tree."

"I thought you didn't drive."

"After my first driving experience, which consisted of smashing Luc's precious Ferrari, I don't. I haven't had the nerve." A tiny smile played at the corners of her mouth. "Thus, the tree with David's Jag."

"So, the two times you've ever driven a car—expensive cars, no less—you wrecked them both?"

"Two for two," she confirmed.

Huh. He made a mental note to check his insurance coverage…and up it. "How did you even manage to get behind the wheel?"

"I waited until he got out to pump the gas, then locked the doors, climbed behind the wheel and took off. Granted, it was a short trip. But I got far enough away that I could escape into the woods before he caught up with me."

Constantine couldn't help himself. He laughed. "You never cease to amaze me."

"To be honest, I'd have preferred a much less amazing night" was her heartfelt reply.

"That makes two of us." To his relief, she'd stopped shivering. "Put your seat back and go to sleep. You'll feel better."

For some reason, his suggestion made her flinch. "If you don't mind, I think I'd like to stay awake."

"Of course I don't mind."

"I just…" She shuddered. "I can't go to sleep. Not after…"

He caught an undercurrent of emotion ripping through her voice—fear—and his hands clenched around the steering wheel. No matter what it took or how long the wait, he would see to it that d'Angelo suffered for his actions. That he never had the opportunity to take advantage of another woman. Constantine hadn't been in a position to ensure it last time. This time he had all the resources he needed. Plus, he had the Dante family behind him. Or he would once they heard his version of what transpired this evening.

She spoke again after a brief silence. "There's something that keeps nagging me about this whole thing."

"Really? There's quite a bit about it that's nagging me," Constantine retorted.

"Why would David want to force me to the altar?"

That stopped him and Constantine turned her question over in his mind, frowning. "What do you mean?"

"He said that he was…" Again the hesitation. "He was compromising me in order to force me into marriage. But I can't figure out why he'd want to do that. What's in it for him?"

Constantine's frown cleared. "That's easy enough. I suspect it has to do with money."

Gianna shook her head. "That can't be it. David has money coming out of his ears."

"Don't be so sure. According to my father, there have been rumors circulating about the source of all that money."

"You're kidding. What sort of rumors?"

"I don't have all the details. But I intend to find out."

"Funny."

Constantine shot her a swift look. "You find something amusing in all this?"

She yawned. "Just that if you're right, David only wanted to marry me because I have money." Her eyes fluttered closed. "And that's the only reason you wouldn't."

"Not the only reason, *piccola*," he said softly.

But despite her decision to remain awake, she'd fallen asleep, fully relaxing for the first time. She remained curled in a ball, snuggled deep into the leather seat. Even with the shallow cuts marring her long legs, they were sleek and shapely beneath the trailing tails of his tux jacket. She'd slicked her damp hair behind her ears, but the humidity caused it to escape in a riot of soft brown and gold curls, framing her scratched face. She looked pale, drawn and exhausted.

And Constantine had never seen a more beautiful sight.

Another few miles down the road she jerked awake with a whimpered cry, bolting upright in her seat. "You're fine," he soothed. "You're safe."

"Sorry, sorry." She shot a hand through her tousled hair. "Did I fall asleep?"

"Do *not* apologize." He struggled to temper the grittiness in his voice with only limited success. Just what she needed. Another male scaring the hell out of her. "Yes, you fell asleep."

"I didn't mean to do that."

"You probably needed it." And she did, despite her residual fear. "We're just coming into the city. I'll have you home in a few more minutes."

She didn't reply, but intense relief speared across her face.

A short time later, Constantine pulled up outside of her row house. Gianna started to open the car door and he stopped her. "Will my Porsche fit in your garage or do you use the space for storage?"

She stared at him blankly. "My garage?"

"I'm staying the night and I don't want to spend the next several hours searching for a legal place to park," he explained patiently. "Will my car fit in your garage?"

He could see the progression of her thoughts written in her expression. Confusion. Dawning comprehension. Stubborn refusal. "That's not necessary."

"D'Angelo is still out there. I'm assuming he was seriously ticked off when he left you. I'm not going to take the chance that he may come by while you're sleeping off the last of whatever he gave you. Your choices are…" He held up a finger. "One. We go to the emergency room and get you checked out. At the very least, they should look at the cuts on your feet."

She instantly shook her head. "There's no need. I'm fine. Like I told you, I didn't get a full dose of the drug."

He refused to let her get away with the lie. "What you mean is… If you tell the doctors what happened, they'll call the police and you want to avoid that particular complication."

She sighed. "Something like that."

"Exactly like that. Fair warning, if those cuts are bad you're going to the emergency room whether you want to or not." He held up a second finger. "Two. I take you to the relative of your choice and you spend the night there."

She immediately shook her head. "You know what will happen if I do."

Yes, he did. "All hell will break loose and—surprise, surprise—they'll insist on calling the police."

"Or, more likely they'll want to take matters into their own hands. I can't risk that happening."

That was going to happen anyway. She just didn't realize it. Yet. He held up another finger. "Three. I come in and spend the night. Someone needs to be available in case you suddenly get sick and need to go to the emergency room.

Or if d'Angelo follows you here, you need someone who can take him down. That would be me, in case you were wondering."

She blew out a sigh. "I sort of figured out that part."

"I'm glad to hear it. So." He lifted an eyebrow. "Which option do you choose?"

"Three," she conceded grudgingly. She fished through her purse and pulled out a key. "There's an automatic garage door opener, but I don't have the controller since I never use it."

Constantine took the key she'd given him and opened the door manually. A short minute later, he had the car parked in the miniscule garage. After locking up, he led the way, making a swift search of her neat-as-a-pin home, one she'd thoroughly stamped with her unique personality.

The colors she'd chosen were as vivid as she was. Strong, bright blues and greens with splashes of lavender, all accented with crisp white trim. She'd blended antiques with contemporary furniture and pulled it off brilliantly. She definitely had an eye for color and balance. If she ever tired of working for Dantes, he could use her in his restoration firm.

He checked each and every room, including closets and beneath furniture. Anyplace a man might hide. He didn't expect to find anyone. The house had an undeniable air of emptiness, but he refused to take any chances with Gianna's safety.

"Do you really think David is hiding under the bed in my guest room waiting to attack me?" she asked near the end of his search, exasperation clear in her voice.

Even after the events of that evening, she still didn't get it. "When it comes to d'Angelo, anything is possible." He could hear the Italian in his voice deepening, thickening.

"Since your safety is paramount, I search the house. The entire house."

She instantly caved. "You're right. Of course you're right."

She trailed behind him, a distracting sight in his shirt and tails. The outfit hung on her slender frame, giving her a vulnerable, disheveled appearance that stirred his most primal protective instincts. She didn't look well, her face even paler than before. Without a word, he headed for her bedroom.

"Do you want a shower before bed?" he asked. "You'd probably feel better. Then I want to take a look at your feet and make sure you don't need stitches."

She pulled a leaf from her hair and wrinkled her nose at it. "My feet are fine. If any of the cuts were bad enough to require stitches I wouldn't be able to walk. That said, I definitely want a shower. I'm filthy and I think I brought half the forest home with me." She folded her arms across her chest, the ends of his tux dribbling off her fingertips. "But I don't want to go to bed."

He fought back a smile. She sounded like a recalcitrant five-year-old. "You're afraid to go to sleep. I understand. But I swear to you, Gianna, I'll keep you safe."

Tears filled her eyes and she stepped into his waiting arms. "It was so close, Constantine."

"Not as close as you might think," he lied, holding her tight against him. She was safe, he reminded himself. And relatively unharmed. "I'd tracked you as far as Calistoga and wasn't too far behind you. I knew d'Angelo owned a lodge near there, and my father was working to get the exact address."

She stilled. "You called Vittorio? He knows what happened?"

"I would have called His Holiness, himself, if I thought

he could have given me d'Angelo's address. Fortunately my father has excellent connections. One way or the other, I would have reached you in time."

Her chin quivered, her jade-green eyes overflowing as emotion set in. "Thank you."

"You're welcome." He released her, nudging her in the direction of the bathroom. "Try not to fall asleep in there, okay?"

She didn't linger. Ten minutes later she emerged, pink-cheeked and smelling subtly of herbs and flowers. She'd wrapped herself in a thick, velour robe. After checking her feet and finding only minor cuts and bruises, he turned down the bed while she stripped off the robe and climbed between the sheets. He lifted an eyebrow at the thigh-length cotton shift she wore beneath. With the light behind her, it was practically transparent. He kept his eyes off the press of feminine curves thrusting against the thin cotton, all the while fighting to maintain an ironclad hold on his libido.

"I think I'd like to leave the light on," she said, pulling the covers up to her chin.

"That's fine." He indicated a heavily cushioned chaise lounge chair covered in antique-rose velvet. "I'll be right here if you need me."

She frowned. "Don't be ridiculous, Constantine. You'll never get to sleep on that. It's way too small. Use the guest room."

"I'm staying right here." His voice brooked no opposition. He held up his hand when she would have argued. "You'll sleep better, *piccola,* having someone close by. And I'll sleep better having you where I can keep watch over you."

She examined the chair again, then him. "Are you sure?"

"Positive. Knowing that all I have to do is open my eyes and see you, safe and sound, will put me right out."

Tears filled her eyes again. "Thank you, Constantine," she said in a husky voice. "You have no idea—" She broke off and shook her head.

"I think I do." He approached and, using the utmost restraint, kissed her forehead. "Try to sleep."

She did, which came as a huge relief to Constantine. He waited until she was deeply unconscious, then slipped from the room and placed a call. When he finished, he returned to the bedroom. He paused at the foot of the bed, gazing at Gianna, and made a silent vow.

No matter what it took, he'd keep this woman safe from harm. He knew that part of the drive to protect came from this peculiar Inferno which connected them, the link so strong it didn't give him any other option. But it went much deeper than that. When she hurt, he hurt. When she hungered, he felt the need to feed her. What gave her joy, he was driven to provide for her. Her wants and his were so tightly bound that they were almost indistinguishable.

Even as he acknowledged those binds, they chafed, stealing his independence. He hadn't asked for this connection. And though he wanted Gianna, he didn't want to be controlled by her. It felt unnatural.

Well, that would change soon enough.

What David d'Angelo had set out to accomplish would happen, just with a different man. Instead of d'Angelo being honor-bound to take Gianna as his bride, Constantine would be the one. Oh, his bride-to-be wouldn't be pleased with his ruthlessness. But she hadn't given him any other choice. She'd inflicted him with The Inferno, infecting him with its fever and desperation. Then she'd had the unmitigated gall to change her mind and allow d'Angelo to come within inches of harming her.

Now she'd deal with the consequences. Her family would take care of the problem from this point forward, sweep them up in an unbreakable net of demand and propriety and cart them to the altar—willingly or not.

And then he would be in charge of The Inferno. He would find a way to douse the fire. At the very least, he'd wield the flames instead of suffering from the constant burn of its touch.

Gianna woke a few hours later with a panicked gasp, swimming to the surface from a terrifying nightmare landscape filled with monsters and screaming tires and bogs of quicksand that sucked at her legs and prevented her from fleeing from some unseen threat. Before she'd shuddered out a single breath, Constantine joined her on the bed, pulling her into the warm protection of his embrace.

"Easy now," came his steadying voice. "You're safe. He can't get to you."

His mouth drifted across the top of her head in the lightest of caresses. Reassuring. Passionless. Compassionate. Although she appreciated the reassurance and compassion, she didn't want passionless. She wanted to feel something other than fear. She curled tight against his bare chest. His warmth surrounded her, easing her bone-deep chill, while the calm, steady beat of his heart soothed her.

"Nightmare," she explained through chattering teeth. "Bad."

"I gathered." She thought he might have feathered another kiss across the top of her head, though she couldn't be certain. But it gave her hope. "It's not real," he soothed.

"I know. At least, part of me knows. The other part—"

She broke off with a shrug. Unable to help herself she pressed closer, sliding her arms around his waist and clinging. To her relief, he didn't push her away, though she sensed a serious internal debate raging. Not that she cared. She was scared and alone, and tired of being both. It wasn't a case of "any port in a storm." She needed Constantine. Only Constantine.

"Stay with me," she whispered.

He swore in Italian, a soft, intently masculine comment that under other circumstances would have made her laugh. "Gianna, this is dangerous."

"I'm not asking you to make love to me."

"I may not be able to help myself."

"You're not David."

He stiffened. "No, I'm definitely not d'Angelo. But I'm still a man. You're vulnerable right now. It's late and I'm tired. And you're not wearing many clothes. For that matter, neither am I." He adopted a reasonable tone. "Admit it, Gianna. Given our reaction to each other, it's a volatile combination."

True. That didn't change anything. "I swear I won't take advantage of you." To her relief, he released a snort of laughter. "But right now I need someone to hold me."

He sighed. "I should have taken you to your parents."

"Probably," she conceded. "Since you didn't, you're stuck with me."

He hesitated, then nodded. "Fine. Lie down."

She did as he requested. To her surprise, he jerked the covers up to her chin so she was completely cocooned, then slid an arm around her while he remained on top of the sheet and blanket.

"Seriously?" she asked.

"Seriously." The metaphorical—or maybe not so metaphorical—immovable object. "Now go to sleep. It'll be daylight in another few hours."

"Would you do one more thing for me?"

"Are you hungry? Thirsty?"

"No." She leaned into him, doing her best to be an

irresistible force. In her case, definitely not a metaphorical one. "Would you kiss me good-night?"

"You are determined to test the limits of my self-control." He spoke in Italian, a dead giveaway.

"Would you rather David was the last man to have kissed me?"

It was the wrong thing to say. Absolutely. Totally. The. Wrong. Thing.

The soft light from the bedside table cut across the rigid lines of his face, striking off the hard planes and sinking into the harsh angles. He gazed down at her, his eyes black crystals of barely suppressed emotion, anger in the foreground, hot desire glittering behind. He said something else in Italian, the words fighting each other. Biting words that came too fast for her to catch. Not that she needed to understand each and every word. The underlying message came through loud and clear.

Constantine wasn't a man to taunt.

He moved so fast she never saw it coming, stripping away the covers and baring her to his gaze. He took his time, looking his fill. The cotton shift she wore provided next to no protection, the fabric so sheer it revealed more than it concealed, hugging her feminine curves and misting his view just enough to make it all the more enticing.

He took his time, studying the generous curve of her breasts, the nipples tight coral peaks thrusting against the cotton and betraying the extent of her hunger. He noticed. Of course he noticed. How could he not? His gaze wandered lower, across her belly which quivered in reaction. Lower still. To the soft brown shadow at the apex of her thighs.

He lifted his hand and for a split second she thought he'd touch her. That he'd rip off her nightshift the way he'd ripped off her gown in the gas station parking lot. Her breath caught and held, waiting for that touch. It never came. Instead his hand hovered a scant inch above her, before following the same path as his gaze. He splayed his fingers, heat pouring from his palm and burning through her shift. Not once did he touch her, though her body reacted as though he had.

She waited for the acrid wash of fear to sweep over her. But it never did. Hunger and want—those existed without question. So did a keen edge of pleasure. Her breasts felt painfully full, lush and acutely sensitive. A heaviness invaded the very core of her, loosening and softening and ripening. A woman preparing for the possession of her mate.

One emotion was lacking.

"No fear," she murmured in relief. "None at all."

He froze. "This is a mistake."

She smiled. Hell, she beamed. She was just so thankful that Constantine could look at her with such intense desire without it sparking flashes of David. "A lovely mistake." She caught his hand in hers, guiding it to her body. "Touch me," she whispered. "Touch me the way a man is meant to touch a woman."

And then he did. As though unable to help himself, he trailed a finger from the juncture between neck and shoulder downward over the slope of her breast. Her nipples pressed against the cotton, so tight she almost couldn't bear it. He hooked a finger in the neckline of her shift and nudged it down just enough to expose them. Gently, sweetly, he took the first into his mouth and caressed it with tongue and teeth. A cry caught in the back of her throat, a keening sound of intense pleasure. Then he turned his attention to the other.

Her head tipped back and the breath shuddered from her lungs, his name escaping on a moan of delight. She slid her fingers deep into the heavy waves of his hair and held him close. "How can this be a mistake?"

He lifted away from her, ignoring her attempts to pull him back into her embrace. Then he waited, allowing the tension to build. Stillness settled over them both, their breath harsh in the silence of the night. Then, slowly, oh, so slowly, he cupped her head. Little by little he leaned in until their lips were no more than a breath apart.

Then he erased even that bit of space. He kissed her, eradicating all memory of everything and everyone who'd gone before. He took his time, the kiss slow and potent and deliciously thorough. She responded, helpless to resist. And why should she? She wanted this as much as he did. Maybe even more. She'd waited for months. Nearly two full years. She refused to wait another minute.

"Make love to me," she urged.

To her distress, he shook his head. "That's not going to happen, Gianna."

"But—"

He stopped her with another kiss that had every thought seeping from her head except what he was doing to her and how he did it. "D'Angelo drugged you tonight," he murmured between leisurely, sampling tastes. "It's likely that you're still feeling the effects."

"I'm not. I swear I'm not."

"You were drugged, attacked. Terrorized. Still in shock." She wished she could deny his catalog of events, but she couldn't. "And you just woke from a nasty nightmare. That makes you vulnerable, and I don't take advantage of vulnerable women."

"Even if the vulnerable woman in question says it's okay? Because that's what I'm saying. Okay. Go right ahead. I'm all yours." He was killing her. "Please, Constantine."

"Would you have me compromise my sense of honor?" he countered.

She closed her eyes. "Considering how I feel right now? Yes, yes I would." An inner debate raged, one that filled her with frustration. Damn it, she'd been a Dante for too long, knew all too well the importance of honor. She continued to debate for another full minute while he waited her out. Then she caved. "When you put it like that…"

"There's no other way *to* put it."

She couldn't argue, not about an issue as serious as a man's honor. It wasn't something the Dantes took lightly, any more than the Romanos. "Will you still hold me?"

"That I can do." He covered her again and settled in beside her. Pulling her into his arms, he just held her. "Better?"

"Frustrating."

He chuckled. "That makes two of us." He kissed her with unmistakable finality. She could still feel the edge of desire, banked, but white-hot around the edges. "Go back to sleep. And this time, try not to press my buttons."

She yawned. "Push your buttons. And I wasn't."

"No? I seem to remember you throwing David in my face. You didn't just press my button. Or even push it. You kicked it with those spiked heels you love to wear."

"Maybe." Honesty forced her to concede, "Okay, definitely."

"Don't do it again. Not with d'Angelo."

She looked at him curiously. "David said the two of you had a history."

Tension speared across the muscles in Constantine's jaw. "Is that what he called it?"

"What would you call it?"

"Funny. I'd have said you were in a better position to answer that question."

She stiffened. "I don't understand. What do you mean?"

"How would you describe what he attempted to do tonight?"

She didn't want to say the word. Couldn't. It would make it too real. She moistened her lips. "After you rescued me... You said he'd done this before. I'd forgotten until just now."

"The drug will do that to you."

"Who else did he drug? Who did he do this to before me?"

"Ariana."

Five

Gianna bolted upright in bed. "Oh, no. Oh, Constantine, no. Not Ariana."

"It's all right. I found her—"

She burst into tears. "How could it be all right? He… he…" She fought to get the words out. "She would have been terrified when she returned from Italy and saw me with him. I'd never have gone out with him if I'd known. And I'd have made him pay for hurting her. I swear I would have. Somehow. Someway."

"Calm down, Gianna." Constantine lifted onto his elbow and smoothed her hair back from her face. "She wouldn't have been terrified when she saw the two of you together for one simple reason. Unlike you, she consumed all of the drug d'Angelo gave her. She has no memory of the events of that night. Not being drugged. Not of how close she came to disaster. Not of my arriving in time to save her. I saw no reason to tell her the sordid details then, or mention it since. She was barely seventeen."

"Seventeen?" Tears slipped down Gianna's cheeks. "So, he didn't…?" She couldn't say the word.

"No. I got there in time. She barely even remembers d'Angelo."

Something else clicked. David's opening salvo at the Midsummer Night's gala when he'd first spoken to Constantine. "That's what he meant about your timing."

Constantine nodded. "I wasn't in a position to make him pay with Ariana. But I swear to you, he won't get away with it again."

"What happened? To Ariana, I mean?"

"Come." He eased her back into his arms and she surrendered to the embrace, using his warmth to comfort her distress. "I'll tell you the story if you promise to go to sleep afterward."

"I promise." Honesty forced her to add, "If I can."

"You have to understand something that is very uncomfortable for me to speak of."

He'd switched to Italian again, his voice stiff with pride and something else. Pain? "Something from your past?" she hazarded a guess.

"It has to do with the manner in which I was raised."

"Old Italian aristocracy?"

"That's at the root of it, yes. The Romanos have the name, but not the money to go with it. We own the land and the palazzo, but have no way to maintain it. Because it has been in our family for so many generations, it would be sacrilege to sell. So we struggle over money."

"Why not get a job?"

Constantine laughed without humor. "You and I think alike. Unfortunately my father considered this beneath him. We are only recently poor. My grandfather made some unfortunate investments and my father finished the job with other bad choices. More than anything, I wished to start up my own business. But there was no capital. No seed money. I attended Oxford. My grandmother—she wrote the Mrs. Pennywinkle children's books before Ariana took over. You are familiar with Mrs. Pennywinkle?"

"Sure. I loved her stories as a child." They were beautifully illustrated tales, all about a china doll named Nancy who passed from needy child to needy child. With each subsequent owner came exciting adventures and heartrending problems for whichever youngster came into possession of the doll. By the end of the book, Nancy had helped resolve the child's problems and magically moved on to the next boy or girl in need. "I even owned a Nancy doll. It was one of my favorite toys growing up."

"My grandmother, Penelope, paid for my education with the royalty money she earned from them. But I could not take her money to start up my business. It would have been—"

"Dishonorable?"

He slanted her a swift, hard look. "Are you making fun of me?"

"Not even a little," she instantly denied. "I'm in total sympathy with you. Our family also went through a period of financial difficulty."

"I vaguely remember Babbo telling me about that. It involved your uncle Dominic, didn't it?"

"Yes. He made some unwise investments, expanded into other areas of the business too fast, and nearly put Dantes out of business. Since my father never handled any of the financial aspects of the business, he had no idea how to turn things around. Like Luc, he dealt with the security end of things. So, after Uncle Dominic's death, Sev stepped in and salvaged the business. It was a point of honor that he make up for his father's mismanagement. But it was touch and go there for a while and we had to sell off almost all of Dantes except for the main jewelry business. It took Sev years to buy back all we'd lost."

"Then you do understand." He hesitated. "This brings me to the d'Angelos."

She made the connection. "They're bankers. They were in a position to loan you money for Romano Restoration."

Darkness descended. "Yes. D'Angelo and I met at Oxford. I had the name. He had the money. I didn't think anything of it. We were…" He shrugged. "Friends. Or I thought we were. I didn't realize at the time that he deliberately set out to cultivate a friendship. He liked bragging about his close relationship with a Romano."

"I assume at some point he met Ariana."

"It happened on a vacation we took with the d'Angelos when Ariana was in her early teens." There was something in his voice when he said that, something unbearably painful and forbidding. Something he wasn't telling her. "At first, I didn't think anything of it. When I looked at my sister, I saw a child. D'Angelo saw a toy that he didn't yet own. And he needed to own all the toys."

She thought about David's Jag and Rolex and suite at the Ritz. "He still does."

"I'm not surprised." Constantine scrubbed a weary hand across his face. "At some point, d'Angelo made a comment about dating Ariana and I came on like the typical big brother. She was too young, the differences in their ages too great."

"I gather that didn't stop David."

"Not at all. If anything, it made him want her all the more."

"Because she was forbidden fruit."

"Yes. It caused a rift between us. I began to really look

at him, listen to him. When I did, I heard rumors about d'Angelo and women. Ugly rumors that perhaps not all the women were willing. I learned afterward that d'Angelo's father kept it all hushed up with huge payoffs."

Constantine trailed a finger along her arm. He did it in an absentminded manner, not really paying attention to his actions. The featherlight caress sent desire cascading through her and she shut her eyes, fighting to focus on the story instead of his touch.

"What happened then?" Gianna managed to ask.

"By this time we'd become somewhat estranged. But one day he came to me unexpectedly and offered to arrange an interview with his father. He said Aldo was extremely interested in financing my start-up restoration business. It surprised me. But hell, I'd talked about it for years. I thought perhaps d'Angelo extended the offer as an olive branch." He hesitated. His mouth compressed and he shook his head. "I'm deluding myself. I went along because I wanted the opportunity so badly—"

"Stop it, Constantine." She wouldn't allow him to shoulder so much of the blame. "David is responsible for his own choices, not you."

He didn't argue the point, but she didn't think she'd convinced him that he didn't bear some fault in what happened. "A time was set," he continued the narrative, "and I showed up in my best suit, prospectus in hand, my sales pitch polished. David should have been there, but I wasn't too surprised when he wasn't."

"Why not?"

"His family is—or maybe was—ridiculously wealthy. He didn't need to work and invented as many excuses as possible to avoid it. Still, as my former friend and considering he'd set up the interview—"

"You expected David to be there."

"Yes." Constantine closed his eyes, all emotion draining from his voice. For some reason the very lack of emotion made the telling that much worse. "At some point I asked where he was and Aldo gave this laugh."

"Oh, no."

"I knew then. Aldo realized he'd given the game away and told me to let it go. That he'd make it worth my while. That it was only a little fun between consenting adults."

"How many teeth did you knock out?"

A cold smile slashed across Constantine's mouth. "Only one. It took me forever to track down my former friend. I arrived just in time."

"Ariana doesn't remember any of this?"

"Nothing of that night, no. Despite my attempts to hush it up, she later found out that David and some of his friends took bets to see who'd be the first to have her. Fortunately, whoever told her the tale prettied up the details somewhat. She assumed that d'Angelo and his friends were trying to make her fall in love with one of them in order to relieve her of her virginity. She thinks it was because of her name and status."

"That's bad enough."

"True. But the actuality would have been far worse. He wanted her. But more than that, he wanted to hurt me. I could never have lived with myself if Ariana had found out that d'Angelo attempted to get back at me for ending our friendship by using her to make his point."

Gianna rested her hand on his arm, feeling his muscles clench beneath her fingers. "I think it was more than making a point. He may have money, but you have something he could never hope to possess. Honor. Ethics. And a name that stood for just that. I suspect David couldn't stand the idea of your possessing something he didn't. Something he could never possess." Constantine didn't respond and she sensed she'd missed something. It only took a moment's thought to key in on it. "It's not your fault. You must realize that by now. You couldn't have known David had an ulterior motive."

She'd guessed right. Fury tore through him. "That's just it, Gianna. I knew him. I should have known, or at least suspected what he might do. I'll never forgive myself for putting my own selfish interests ahead of my duty and responsibility to Ariana. If I hadn't been so desperate to gain financing for my business, I'd have guessed what d'Angelo was up to."

"You did figure out what David was up to. And you rescued Ariana, just like you rescued me." She pressed her fingertips to his mouth. "Before you say it, you're also not to blame for tonight. You had no way of knowing that he would act so fast. If it's anyone's fault, it's mine. I should have listened to my instincts…and to you."

He kissed her fingertips. Then he leaned in and kissed her. She surrendered to the embrace, helpless to resist. How could she have ever thought she'd someday feel this sort of desire for David? It either existed or it didn't.

It was like The Inferno. Some people melded, driven together by forces beyond their control. Others didn't. And even though she knew that Constantine wasn't the only man capable of sparking The Inferno, she'd never felt it with anyone else. Did it really matter that he didn't experience it the way she did? That for him, there'd been a glitch in the connection, enabling him to walk away from her? Couldn't she be happy with what he was willing to give her?

He deepened the kiss and she moaned in longing. Why couldn't he want her as much as she wanted him? As though to prove the point, he pulled back and brushed her hair behind her ear.

"Sleep now," he said.

"Yeah, right. I'm sure your bedtime story will put me right off."

"Try." A slow smile played at the corner of his mouth. "For the sake of my sanity, please try."

"Well, when you put it like that…"

She closed her eyes, if only to shut out the sight of him. And though she didn't think she'd sleep, the instant she snuggled against him, she went under.

A loud pounding woke Gianna the next morning. She bolted upright in bed, disoriented. Confusion battled with a sudden, overwhelming alarm, made worse by the empty indentation beside her.

"Constantine?" His name escaped, edged with panic.

"Right here."

At some point he'd left the bed and returned to the chaise. At the commotion emanating from below he stood, looking strong and rested despite all they'd been through the night before. His air of calm immediately relaxed her. He still wore the trousers from his tux, but hadn't bothered to don the shirt or jacket he'd loaned her the night before, possibly because she'd left them in a heap in the corner of the bathroom.

She vaguely recalled hearing him in the shower at some point in the early hours of the morning, though a dark shadow clung to his jaw indicating he hadn't borrowed a razor, and his hair fell across his brow in heavy, unruly waves. Despite that, his "morning after" look made him almost unbearably appealing.

He checked his watch. "Don't get up. I'll see who it is."

"What if it's David?"

He didn't hesitate. "Then he'll soon regret ever coming near you."

She despised the wave of fear that swept through her when she thought about David. She'd never experienced that before. Nor had she ever considered herself weak or vulnerable. He'd stolen her innate feeling of security and, for that alone, she'd never forgive him. As for the rest, she'd find some way to make him pay for drugging her, for attempting to assault her. Because there wasn't a doubt in her mind he would have done precisely that if she hadn't gotten away.

Determined not to surrender to cowardice, she tossed aside the covers and swept up her robe. She tied the sash around her waist in a quick, angry motion, then followed Constantine from the bedroom. He opened the front door just as she reached the foyer. To her horror, Primo stood there, his gaze moving from a half-dressed Constantine to Gianna in her bathrobe, bare feet and bed-head hair.

Uh-oh. This couldn't be good.

"May I come in?" Primo asked, excruciatingly polite.

Gianna thrust her hands through her hair in an effort to smooth the unruly curls. Not that it helped. It simply drew attention to the horror of it all. "Of course. We…I wasn't expecting you."

"This I can see."

"I'll start a pot of coffee," Constantine said, and disappeared in the direction of the kitchen.

She didn't know which was worse. The fact that he'd deserted her. Or the fact that—from her grandfather's perspective—he was familiar enough with her home to fix the coffee. Not that he was. But it certainly must seem that way to Primo. Warmth burned her cheeks and she avoided his gaze.

She trailed after Constantine like a caboose on a runaway train, helpless to prevent it from careening onward to its predetermined destination. She didn't have a hope in hell of preventing the coming disaster. Still, she was driven to try. "Just so you know, this isn't what it looks like," she said, in an attempt to divert the impending train wreck.

"It looks like Constantine has spent the night."

Gianna reddened. Sharp curve ahead! "Well, yes, he did. But not the way you mean."

"And which way is that, *chiacchierona?*" he asked gently.

"He…we…I—"

"Cream? Sugar?" Constantine interrupted.

Primo waved aside the offer. "Black. And strong enough to grow hair on my chest. At my age I could use some."

Gianna decided to give up on trying to explain the situation to her grandfather. There was no excuse Primo would find acceptable to explain Constantine spending the night with her. "Please don't take this the wrong way," she said to him. "But what are you doing here?"

"Constantine called me."

Shock froze her in place for an instant as her train jumped the track and completely derailed. She stood amidst the carnage and swung an outraged look in Constantine's direction. "You. Called. *Primo?*" Didn't he understand the ramifications of that?

Apparently he didn't because he appeared neither concerned, nor the least apologetic. "Yes. I explained about d'Angelo. It was my duty."

"Now that Constantine is your fiancé, it is only proper that he discuss such matters with me," her grandfather informed her. He turned his attention to Constantine. "I have made some phone calls. My understanding is that d'Angelo has left the country. The claim is urgent business."

"I'm not surprised."

Primo nodded in agreement. "Nor am I."

Gianna held up her hands. "Wait a minute. Wait just one

darn minute here. Could we forget about David? If he's left the country, he's not of immediate concern."

"He's of concern to me," Constantine retorted.

"I am also concerned," Primo added with a nod.

She refused to allow them to sidetrack her. Her gaze narrowed on her grandfather. "First, Constantine is *not* my fiancé. And second, it was my place to tell you about last night, not his. I'm not some delicate piece of china to be placed on a shelf while the men take care of business. I'm a woman in charge of her own destiny."

Primo gestured toward Gianna's mug. "More sugar," he instructed Constantine. "And for the sake of your marriage, I warn you to avoid conversation with our Gianna until after she has had a full cup of sweet coffee. Better if it is two."

She gritted her teeth to keep from saying something she'd regret. "Primo—"

"*Ascoltare me,* Gianna Marie Fiorella."

"Little flower?" Constantine murmured, his eyes filled with laughter. "Somehow I never thought of you that way."

She shot him a smoldering look before returning her attention to Primo. "I'm listening."

Her grandfather's index finger thumped against the table. "In the eyes of your family, you are engaged to this man. He proposed to you last night in front of us all. And he has now spent the night with you."

"But we didn't—"

"He was in your bed?"

Color burned across her cheekbones. "Primo," she muttered.

"I'll take that as a yes." He nodded as though that sealed the deal and drank a long swallow of coffee. "I will speak to the priest and discuss dates while you and your mother attend to such matters as the dress and flowers. Your babbo will have a conversation with Constantine about his duties as a husband. Are we clear on this matter?"

She waited a split second to see if Constantine planned to say something helpful. Anything. Apparently he didn't, since he simply stretched out his long legs and buried his smile in the steam rising from his coffee mug. Gianna shot to her feet, tightening the belt of her robe with a swift jerk that nearly cut off her circulation.

Fine. She'd just claimed she was a woman in charge of her own destiny. Time to prove it. "I understand why you think we should marry, Primo. But you can't force me to the altar." She glared at Constantine. "None of you can. I'm not Luc and Téa to be threatened into a marriage I don't want."

"Who says you don't want it?" Constantine spoke up for the first time. "You know perfectly well this is where our relationship has been heading. There was never any doubt about that."

"*What* relationship?" she shot back. "We felt a few sparks. Exchanged a few kisses. But we don't know anything about each other. Certainly not enough for marriage."

"You have felt The Inferno with this man?" Primo broke into the conversation.

She'd never been able to lie to her grandfather. She doubted she'd be able to this time, either. She came as close as she could manage. "Maybe."

Constantine held out his right hand, palm up. "Definitely. We felt it the first time we touched." At Primo's lifted brow, he added, "Ariana's wedding."

"So many months ago?" her grandfather marveled. "And you have not acted in all this time? How is this possible?"

Gianna stabbed a finger in Constantine's direction. "My point exactly. How can it be The Inferno? If it were, he never could have stayed away. Certainly not this long."

A hint of anger sparked in Constantine's gaze and he slowly climbed to his feet, towering over her. "You know damn well why I stayed away." It was a darn good thing she could speak Italian considering he used it every time he got angry. Which, it would seem, was often. "I had no choice."

"You did have a choice. You *chose* to stay away," she retorted, folding her arms across her chest. She didn't care if it made her look defensive. She felt defensive.

"Chose?" Anger flashed, caught fire. "I had nothing to offer but my name."

"That would have been more than enough for me," she retorted.

"It would have dishonored me to live off my wife's money and provide nothing in return," he shot back. "For the past nineteen months I have worked day and night to build a business. And I succeeded. I succeeded well enough to move here. Did I ask you to come to me in Italy? No. Because I know how much your family means to you. Instead I opened my business in San Francisco so we would have each other *and* your family. And what do you tell me when I arrive?" Fury ripped through his voice. "You tell me you've moved on. *Moved on!*"

"It had been nearly two years," she protested. "Was I supposed to wait forever?"

He kept going as though she'd never interrupted. "You had moved on to that bastard d'Angelo. A man without scruples, without honor. A man who tried to drug you in order to force you into marriage."

"If he'd succeeded—" and just the thought had her breaking out in a cold sweat "—I would have told him the same thing I'm telling you. I won't be forced into marriage. Not by anyone, for any reason."

"I don't understand. If you don't want marriage, then

what the hell *do* you want from me, Gianna?" Constantine demanded. "Why am I here? Or have these past nineteen months been a waste of my time?"

Good question. She planted her hands on her hips and spared her grandfather a swift glance. He continued to drink his coffee, watching the drama unfolding with an expression of utter delight. Honestly. There were times her family drove her crazy. She looked at Constantine uncertainly. "Are you interested in marriage?"

He swore. "Why do you think I returned? Why do you think I'm listening to this craziness instead of carting you off to bed and spending the next week compromising you so thoroughly you'll have no choice but to marry me?"

Color darkened her cheeks. This time she didn't dare look at her grandfather, though she heard his soft, choked laughter. She held up her hands. "Enough, already. If you're serious about a relationship, then you'll have to go about it the normal way. The old-fashioned way."

That stopped him. "What are you talking about?"

Exasperated, she said, "I'm talking about dating, Constantine. I'm talking about going out to dinner and getting to know each other. Learning each other's likes and dislikes. Figuring out whether or not we're actually compatible." She shoved her palm in his direction and shook it at him. "This isn't any guarantee of happiness. I happen to know that for a fact."

Silence reigned at the end of her tirade.

"Exactly how do you know this for a fact, *chiacchierona?*" Primo asked, the question dropping into the abrupt silence.

Oh, no. She refused to go there. Refused to share the secret she'd kept since her thirteenth birthday. Her entire family believed implicitly in The Inferno, believed that it was permanent and everlasting. No way would she be the one to disabuse them of a legacy they celebrated and cherished.

She folded her arms across her chest and—for once in her life—closed her mouth and kept it closed.

To her profound relief, Constantine inadvertently came to her rescue. "Gianna has a point," he offered, albeit reluctantly. "Even though we've known each other for more than a year and a half, we've only been together for a handful of days."

"What do you suggest?" Primo asked.

"Time," Gianna immediately replied. "Time for the two of us to become better acquainted. To look before we leap."

Primo didn't want to agree, she could see it in the brilliant gold of his eyes. After a moment's reflection, he nodded, also reluctantly. "Very well. I will say nothing of what I have learned here this morning while I give you this time." He fixed Gianna with a cool, pointed stare. "One month, *chiacchierona*. After that you marry, willing or not, even if I have to carry you down the aisle, myself."

Six

The instant Primo left, Gianna retreated upstairs, no doubt to change. Constantine followed. He wasn't about to give her the opportunity to fortify her barricades or find a loophole buried within Primo's ultimatum.

"I need to change," she informed him the instant he entered her bedroom.

He made himself comfortable on her chaise lounge. "I'm not stopping you."

She turned on him, planting her hands on her hips. "What is it with you? Last night I practically threw myself at you and you wanted nothing to do with me. This morning you won't give me an inch to breathe."

"You have an inch." He eyeballed the distance between them. "By my calculation, you have quite a few inches."

"You know what I mean."

She must have realized he had no intention of leaving. With a sigh of irritation, she spun on her heel and crossed to

her closet, flinging open the door and disappearing inside.
Curious, he followed.

"Madre di Dio," he murmured faintly.

"I don't want to hear a word about it," she retorted, her
back to him.

He thought he caught a defensive edge in her voice. "Just
out of curiosity, how many pairs of shoes do you own?" he
asked.

She turned, clutching a pair of heels. "Not enough."
She glanced at the huge rack of tidily shelved shoes which
covered every spectrum of the rainbow. "Besides, they're
not all mine. Some of them are Francesca's. We discovered
a while back that we wear identical sizes."

He folded his arms across his chest. "Should I assume
that if some of these are hers, she has some of yours?"

She waffled for a second, before conceding, "Maybe."

Oh, yeah. Definitely defensive. He examined the closet
and shook his head. "What did you do, convert an adjoining
bedroom into a closet?"

The blush sweeping across her elegant cheekbones gave
him the answer. "Not that it's any of your business," she
muttered.

"It will be when we marry."

She held up a hand. "Okay, stop right there. There is no
'when.' There is only a very shaky 'maybe.'"

He crowded her against a row of silk business suits. "You
heard Primo. You have one month of 'maybe' and then it's
a lifetime of 'when.'"

A deeply feminine confusion crept across her face. "Why
are you going along with this? It's ridiculous."

He fisted his hands around the lapels of her robe and
drew her to him. "You started this, Gianna, when you decided to infect me with The Inferno. You can't blame me
if I finish it. What choice did you leave me?"

Her eyebrows shot up. "Infect?"

He gave it to her straight. "Sometimes it feels like that, particularly since I had no choice in the matter."

"It wasn't deliberate," she insisted. "It's not like I can control it. It just happens."

Well, at least all the Dantes were telling identical stories. "Your brothers said the same thing. I'm not sure I believe them." He watched her closely. "Did you Inferno d'Angelo?"

She shook her head. "Absolutely not."

"And yet, you continued to go out with him."

Her chin shot to a combative angle. "Maybe The Inferno is smarter than I am."

"Maybe it's smarter than both of us."

He reeled her in by the lapel of her robe. They stood shoe-to-bare-toe for an endless moment. Unable to resist, he slanted his mouth over hers and slammed them both into a whirlwind of desire. He still wanted her with a desperation every bit as fierce as when they'd first met. It hadn't diminished. Not over time. Not over distance. And definitely not with her winding her arms around his neck and surrendering herself unconditionally to the embrace. He heard the high heels she held hit the carpeted floor one after the other.

Want exploded between them, hot and heavy. More than anything he wished he could sweep her into his arms, carry her back to bed and make love to her for the rest of the weekend. If he did, it would force her to commit. Her family wouldn't give her any other option.

But then, he'd be no better than David.

Her lips parted beneath his and she made a low, hungry sound that threatened to steal every last vestige of his self-control. He yanked at the knot holding her robe together. Stripping away the binding, he slid his hands beneath the heavy velour and over her shoulders. The robe dropped at their feet, leaving her standing there in nothing but the thin cotton shift she'd worn to bed.

"I want you," he said between fierce, biting kisses. "It eats at me, never going away. Never easing."

"I know, I know. I'm sorry." Her arms tightened around his neck and her head fell back, giving him greater access to the long sweep of throat and shoulder. "It's the same for me. I thought I could push it away or ignore it. But it's too strong."

He hooked his fingers in the bodice of her shift in order to slip it downward at the same instant she pulled back. The thin cotton split, the sound of rending cloth harsh in the confines of the closet. For a split second, they both froze. The tattered remains of her nightie hung from her arms, exposing her breasts and belly. He'd never seen anything more beautiful in his life. He started to reach for her, to touch her.

Then an image of David flashed through his mind. Dear God, what had he been thinking? Swearing, he released her and drew back. Without another word, he turned and stepped from the confines of the closet.

"Get dressed." His voice escaped, low and guttural. "I'll wait for you downstairs."

"Constantine—"

He refused to look back. That way led to disaster. "I'm not David. I swear to you I'm not."

"I know that. Of course I know that." Concern mingled with the frustrated hunger underscoring her words. "You never could be. This was an accident."

He fought for control, fought with every ounce of strength he possessed. "Which is why I'm going downstairs. Before I do something I can't live with afterward."

"But—"

He spun around, pushed to the limit of his endurance. "What are you saying, Gianna? That it's acceptable to sleep with me, but I'm not someone you'll marry?"

She drew back in alarm, clutching the remnants of the shift around herself. "No! Of course I'm not saying that."

"Then what are you saying?"

She closed her eyes. "I want you," she confessed.

"And I want you. But I won't use you like some sort of one-night stand. How could I face Primo if I did that? How could I face your brothers?" He softened his tone. "Let's slow down and do what you suggested. Let's get to know each other better."

She nodded. "Okay."

His mouth curved upward in a dry smile. "As soon as you're dressed we'll leave, since clearly, Primo was right."

"As much as I hate to admit it, he usually is." She glanced at him hesitantly. "And after we leave? What then?"

"We'll get to know each other better."

Her brows shot up. "We're going out on a date?"

"Nothing so formal. I thought I'd show you around Romano Restoration. It took a lot of work to put everything in place without you being any the wiser. But I wished to surprise you by having it fully operational when I arrived. It helped that Ariana was in Italy so she didn't accidentally let it slip." He glanced down at himself and grimaced. "Going to Romano's will also give me the opportunity to change since my apartment is above the office complex."

He didn't dare remain in her bedroom a moment longer. He retreated to the kitchen where he leaned against the counter and drank a second cup of coffee. Maybe it would help him regain his self-control. Because if he planned on spending any time around Gianna, he'd need every bit of it. To his relief, she didn't keep him waiting for more than ten minutes.

She appeared downstairs wearing a casual pair of camel-colored slacks and a cream silk blouse. Not as attractive as the shift, but definitely safer. She'd secured her long, gold-streaked brown hair with a simple clip, the curls rioting down her back in joyous abandon. Her makeup was minimal, a touch of mascara and lipstick. She'd used a heavier hand with the blush, no doubt to hide the lingering paleness resulting from the events of the night before.

"I'm set," she announced brightly. Her gaze swept over him and a broad grin spread across her mouth. "My, aren't you looking…dissolute."

He glanced down at the dress shirt and tux jacket he'd rescued from her bathroom floor. He suspected the wrinkles might be permanent. "It's the new me. I call it my morning-after look. What do you think?"

"Very sexy." She actually sounded like she meant it.

He dumped the dregs of his coffee in the sink and rinsed the mug. Turning, he held out his hand. She didn't hesitate, but laced her fingers through his. Their palms melded and the burn from The Inferno flared to life, creating an undeniable heat, tightening the bond that had been created when they first met. Together they headed for the garage.

A few minutes later they were moving easily through the Sunday morning traffic toward Romano Restoration. He found a parking spot on the street, though he could have used the underground lot that serviced the building. This was just more convenient. They entered through the front door of the office complex and took the private elevator to the floors housing his company.

The doors parted and he gestured for her to take the lead. "Romano Restoration occupies the top four floors plus the building's penthouse suite," he explained. "The lower floors handle the business side of the company—accounting, contracts, that sort of thing. The upper two levels deal with customer relations, and the more creative aspects. like architectural and interior design."

A handful of lights sent a soft glow across the pearl-gray carpet, the cloudy morning leaving the remainder of the floor in silky shadow. Even in the dim light Constantine could see the questions building in Gianna's expression. He kept his distance, careful not to touch her. If he made that mistake again, he wouldn't be able to keep his hands off her. And from there it would be a short, sweet step to making her his in every sense of the word.

"It's very elegant," she offered without hesitation. "I love the openness and the understated elegance. It really showcases your business."

"Thanks." He gestured toward the corner office. "That one's mine."

She immediately crossed to look. "Mmm. Nice." She took a deep breath and swung to face him. He could see her steeling herself to say something, something he wouldn't like. "Just one question…"

He tempted fate by taking a step in her direction and cut straight through to the heart of the matter—the issue that had hovered between them like an angry, black cloud ever since his return. The issue that had driven her into d'Angelo's arms and come so close to ending in disaster.

"Why did I wait so long to return to you?" he asked. "Is that what you want to know?"

The question provoked an immediate reaction. The anguish filling her eyes threatened to snap his control. "You said you'd come back."

"And I did."

She shook her head, her mouth tightening. "It took too long. Far too long."

"I came as soon as I could," he argued.

"You never responded to my emails or phone calls. You actively discouraged our communicating and you flat-out refused to let me visit you in Italy." She stepped closer. "Couldn't we have done that much, at least?"

"I warned you about that. You agreed to it." Didn't she get it? "I didn't dare communicate or visit. I sure as hell couldn't have you with me in Italy. It would have distracted me and I'd never have gotten my business off the ground."

Gianna swept a hand through the air to indicate the plush area around them. "You had time for this, though. You had time to build Romano Restoration into a going concern."

"And why do you suppose I did that?" His accent thickened, just as his voice lowered. Darkened. "Why do you suppose I left you?"

"You said…" Her chin wobbled precariously for a brief instant before she clamped down on the helpless betrayal. "You claimed you weren't in a position to support a wife, but that would change. I understand that you wanted to bring more to our relationship than just a name. I really do get that."

"If you get it, then—"

She cut him off with a swift, chopping sweep of her hand. "You said soon." Anger warred with her tears. "Damn it, Constantine, it's been more than a year and a half. That isn't soon."

He couldn't argue her point. Each month he'd been away from her had felt like a year. "I know, sweetheart. I really do. It couldn't be helped. If there had been any other way—" he stopped her before she could speak "—any other way that I could have lived with, I'd have taken it. Please believe that."

"I just wanted to be with you. We could have found a way, either in Italy or here."

Gianna took another step in his direction, and Constantine clamped down on the clawing need to settle this once and for all in the most basic way possible. "As much as I wanted to be with you, I am not the sort of man who can live off the generosity of others. I watched my—" He broke off, switched gears more roughly than he'd have liked. "I've seen others live that way. But I won't. Ever. You do understand that, don't you?"

Her chin shot upward. "Do I understand that your pride is more important than anything else? You made that abundantly clear."

His anger broke free. "How do you think I spent the past year and a half? When Lazz and Ariana married, I'd just scraped together enough money to launch my company in Firenze. I worked day and night to build a small, modest business into something prosperous enough that I could afford to relocate here. Do you think such a thing happens overnight? Do you think it easy to acquire the contracts necessary to give me the start I needed over here? Do you think I could have accomplished such a thing in nineteen short months if I hadn't funneled every ounce of drive into my business?"

She moved closer still, everything about her impacting like a physical blow. Her sweet scent. Her generous curves. Her staggering beauty. "I could have worked with you," she whispered. "Helped you."

"Distracted me," he corrected. "If I'd had you waiting in my bed I never could have accomplished a tenth of what I've been able to, because I never would have been willing to leave your arms."

She smiled while tears of pain glistened in her green eyes. "Then we would have been poor. But at least we would have been together."

He shook his head. "You must allow me to be a man,

Gianna. You cannot control all things in this relationship."

She stiffened. "What do you mean by that?"

He stared broodingly at his open hand. It never ceased to amaze him that there wasn't a physical brand to mark the presence of this Inferno the Dantes generated. He ran his thumb across his palm in a habitual gesture. It didn't matter how hard he rubbed, he could never erase what had been done to him.

"You started this the first time you touched me," he informed her, holding out the hand she'd infected. "But I intend to finish it."

She stilled, the prey sensing the predator for the first time. "How?"

Daring fate, he closed the remaining distance between them and laced their fingers together, used the pull of The Inferno to draw her in. "You made me yours. You caught me. It doesn't matter whether you still want me or not. You initiated something that can't be stopped with a simple, 'I've changed my mind.' It's too late for that. You will be mine."

Her mouth firmed. "You're right. It is too late. I'm not someone you can simply pick up or set aside when the mood strikes you."

"Did it sound like I was setting you aside when I proposed marriage?"

"You mean at the gala? You consider *that* a proposal of marriage?" she dared to scoff. "That was simply your clever way of removing the competition."

"You mean David?"

"Of course I mean David."

Constantine shook his head. "You know damn well he's not my competitor and never could be."

"We know that *now*," she corrected.

"It still would have been a simple matter to get rid of him without proposing in front of your entire family."

That gave her pause. "How?" she asked, genuinely curious.

He smiled tenderly. "Simply by being with you. David would have seen what everyone else sees whenever you and I are together. The very air around us is on the verge of bursting into flames whenever we touch. It isn't something either of us can hide."

"Try."

"Damn it, Gianna!" He shot a hand through his hair. "What the hell do you want from me?"

"Nothing. I don't want a thing from you."

"And you call me proud." Unable to help himself he swept her into his arms, praying his restraint wouldn't snap. She might end up a bit ruffled and undone, but if he could rein in his self-control, it wouldn't go any further than that. "I have spent endless months working night and day doing everything within my power to get back to you as quickly as possible."

Tears welled in her eyes again. Tears of regret. "It's been so long."

"I know, I know. I'm sorry." He feathered a kiss across her mouth. Unable to resist, he deepened it. "I came back as soon as I could, I swear."

She wound her arms around his neck. "I missed you so much. You have no idea how hurt I was by your silence. There were nights I'd lie in bed and ache for you."

He closed his eyes, her brutally frank words impacting like a blow. "I am so sorry. It was never my intention to hurt you. I have missed you beyond measure. But I am here now. Don't let pride keep us apart any longer."

Finally they had the privacy he needed to allow his hunger loose and he couldn't take advantage of it, not after the promise he'd made to Primo. Or at least, not until Gianna had fully committed to him by allowing him to put his ring on her finger. He settled for another lingering kiss, one filled with promise. Filled with longing. A kiss that teetered on the edge of losing control. Her lips parted and her hands slid from his neck to fork deep into his hair, anchoring him in place. Her moan spoke of endless hunger, urging him to take that next, irrevocable step.

"We can't," he murmured against her mouth. "We need to take our time and do this the right way."

To his relief, humor gleamed in her eyes in place of anger. "Do you think either of us is capable of that?"

"We better be or I'll have a tribe of Dantes willing and able to take me apart."

"I won't tell if you won't."

"Are you saying you're ready to wear my ring? To commit to marriage?" He didn't need to hear her response. "No, I can see from your expression that you're not." He snatched a swift kiss, then set her firmly from him. "Come on. Let's go upstairs. I need to change."

He escorted her to his apartment and left her in the great room with its expansive view of the city while he disappeared in the direction of his bedroom to shave and change. He joined her a short time later and found her studying the 3D replica he'd made of the Diamondt building for his presentation to the family, along with a thick book of drawings and samples that detailed the various aspects of the renovation.

"This is gorgeous," she marveled. "I love how you've melded their name with the updates to the building. Are these beveled diamond panes going to be made from leaded glass?"

"Good eye. There are a lot of leaded glass windows in the older homes in the Seattle area. Since this is an older building, it seemed to suit. We're also planning an immense stained-glass window for the foyer."

"I wish I could see it. I'll bet it's gorgeous."

"We're still negotiating the contract, so unless there's a problem, I won't be going up there until it's ready to be signed. But next time I do, you're welcome to accompany me." Maybe it would even be as his wife, though he was careful not to say as much.

"Thanks. I just might take you up on that."

She studied the building a final few minutes, a frown growing between her brows. That couldn't be good.

"What's wrong?" he asked.

"I'd almost forgotten. It wasn't until I saw this model and the Diamondt name that I remembered," she murmured. She shook her head in annoyance. "It would seem you were right. That drug David gave me affected me more than I realized."

Constantine studied her in growing concern. "What have you remembered?"

"Something David said about a diamond. I was going to ask you about it the minute I saw you." She shuddered. "I hadn't expected my escape to be quite so dramatic or frightening, or I would have thought of it sooner." Her gaze shifted from the model to him. "Have you ever heard of a diamond named Brimstone?"

Figlio di puttana! He fought to keep his voice even. "You might say that. Are you telling me David knows about Brimstone?"

She nodded. "He seemed to think I should, too. In fact, he seemed certain that you either had it in your possession and used it to finance Romano Restoration…or you were marrying me in order to get your hands on it." She tilted her head to one side, pinning him with her jade-green eyes.

"What is Brimstone, other than a fire diamond? And why is David d'Angelo trying so desperately to find it?"

"I suspect he's desperate to find it because it's worth somewhere in the neighborhood of ten million dollars." Constantine shrugged. "Perhaps more. And to answer your other question, Brimstone is the reason your cousin, Lazz, and my sister, Ariana, married, sight unseen. To be honest, it's a long story, and it occurs to me that we missed breakfast." He gestured in the direction of the kitchen. "Why don't we throw something together while I tell you about it."

"Now that you mention it, I'm starving." She followed him into the kitchen and took a moment to explore the generous area. Then she made herself at home, raiding the refrigerator. "Looks like you have ingredients for omelets. And maybe… Yup. Fruit salad?"

"Sounds disgustingly healthy."

She held up a package of bacon and a small wheel of cheese. "Better?"

"Much."

He pitched in to help cut and chop right alongside of her while bacon sizzled in the background. She gestured with her paring knife. "So, go on. You were going to explain about Brimstone. What is it? Where did it come from? David seemed to think it disappeared."

"He's right about that much. It did disappear." Constantine sliced into a peach bursting with juice. "As for the rest of the story… Let's see. Where should I start?"

She spared him a swift grin. "Where all good fairy tales start. Once upon a time…"

"Once upon a time," he repeated obediently. "There was an adorable Italian princess named Ariana, who was the apple of her father's eye. One day, when Princess Ariana was just six years old, a prince from a faraway land came to visit. His name was Lazzaro Dante."

"Seriously?"

"Seriously," Constantine confirmed. "Like all good fairy tales, the instant Ariana and Lazzaro touched, something odd happened between them."

Gianna dropped her knife on the counter and spun to face him, openmouthed. "Are you *kidding* me? They felt The Inferno? At such a young age? I didn't even realize that was possible."

"According to my father it was an incipient form of The Inferno. But, yes. Something sparked between them. For some reason, Dominic went insane when he realized what was happening and demanded that he and my father create a marriage contract. He wanted to ensure that my sister and your cousin were strongly encouraged to marry once they were older."

"No way."

He lifted an eyebrow. "No one ever told you any of this?"

Her eyes narrowed in displeasure. "Uh, no. And trust me, someone will pay for that oversight. All I heard was that they felt The Inferno when they met in Italy and decided to marry."

"Ah, but they never actually met in Italy. That was merely the story they put out to explain their whirlwind wedding so that your grandparents and my grandmother wouldn't find out about the contract and the true reason for their marriage. They needed to wed quickly in order to fulfill the terms of the contract."

Gianna picked up her knife again. "Okay, now you've lost me."

"There was a stipulation in the contract that the two must marry by Ariana's twenty-fifth birthday. When the contract came to light they negotiated the marriage by phone and email. They never even met until the actual wedding ceremony."

"But, that's…that's barbaric," she sputtered. "You're telling me they *had* to get married because of some contract your father and Uncle Dominic signed? Why didn't they just tear it up?"

He hesitated. "There may have been a small incentive that made it worthwhile for all parties involved."

Comprehension dawned, turning her eyes a brilliant shade of green. "Brimstone."

Constantine nodded. "Dominic knew about my family's financial issues. So, he offered to give my family half of Brimstone when Lazz and Ariana married."

"And if they didn't marry?"

"Brimstone would be thrown into the ocean and neither family would profit."

"Dear God," Gianna said faintly. "From barbaric to insane."

"You and I think alike, *piccola*. My father, who might be barbaric about some things, is not the least insane when it comes to financial opportunities. He jumped at the offer." Constantine couldn't prevent a hint of bitterness from crawling into his voice. "After all, what did he have to lose?"

"Oh, Constantine," she murmured.

He focused on decapitating strawberries, using a shade more force than strictly necessary. "Not to worry. As it turned out, we never did succeed in selling Ariana off. Though the two married, when the time came to turn over Brimstone, we discovered the diamond had gone missing."

Gianna smothered a laugh. "You'd have thought Lazz

and Ariana would make sure they knew where the diamond was before going to all the trouble of marrying."

Constantine's mouth tightened. "My father didn't inform Ariana of the disappearance until moments before she walked down the aisle. None of the Dantes realized it was missing. You see, Dominic made the mistake of leaving the diamond in my father's safekeeping. I gather it was part of the contract negotiations. As it turned out, Gran... My Grandmother Penelope—"

"The author of the Mrs. Pennywinkle books?"

"That's the one," he confirmed. "She overheard Babbo and Dominic talking about the contract. She was outraged by what they planned."

"As any normal person would be."

"Agreed."

Finished with the fruit salad, he started a pot of coffee, then leaned against the counter and watched Gianna sauté onions, spinach and mushrooms in olive oil. She poured the egg mixture she'd prepared into a pan and added the sautéed vegetables, topping them with a sprinkling of bacon.

"Anyway," he continued, "she stole Brimstone from my father and sewed it into a Nancy doll."

"I used to own a Mrs. Pennywinkle Nancy doll." Gianna snapped her fingers. "Maybe it's in my doll."

"Doubtful. She placed it into the original Nancy doll. The prototype. Ariana gave the doll away to a needy child shortly after she married Lazz."

Gianna's eyes widened. "Oh, dear. I gather she didn't know Brimstone was inside?"

"She didn't have a clue," Constantine confirmed. "By then, she and Lazz had fallen in love and decided to let fate determine where it ended up."

She smiled softly. "How romantic."

"Foolish," he corrected.

She shrugged. "A matter of opinion. Though I can understand your family's disappointment at the loss." A sudden thought occurred. "Just out of curiosity, would you have taken the money from the diamond to start up Romano Restoration?"

He hesitated. "I would have been seriously tempted. But in the end…" He shook his head. "It still would have been money I'd neither earned, nor deserved to profit from. So, no. If the Romanos had taken our share of Brimstone, it wouldn't have changed the past nineteen months, if that's what you're asking. We'd still have been apart."

"Damn it," she whispered.

"What?"

She frowned at him in open displeasure. "I'm beginning to see your point of view in all this. It's really annoying, too."

Amusement combined with a deep tenderness and affection. He loved her honesty and frankness. Loved that she didn't pull her punches, even on those occasions when they stood on opposite sides of the proverbial fence. It also pleased him that she considered the Brimstone contract as much an outrage as he did. He found it encouraging that they were so closely aligned on certain issues. Which reminded him…

"Let's not forget the original problem."

It only took her a moment to follow his line of thought and she winced. "David."

"Yes. Unfortunately d'Angelo has excellent inside information. He knows that Brimstone is missing."

"Not really. He only suspects."

"But once he decides neither family has it—"

"He's going to try to find it," Gianna finished his sentence for him. She expertly folded the omelets, then plated them, grating cheese over the top for the finishing touch. "I wonder if David knows Brimstone is sewn into one of the dolls. I'd hate to think he's running around gutting every poor Nancy doll he can find in a frantic search for the diamond."

Constantine grimaced, gathering the necessary items to set the table. "Hell, I hadn't considered that possibility."

"Maybe we should. And maybe we should find out where the diamond went before he does." She busied herself filling two bowls with fruit salad while she considered. "One final question."

"Just one?"

She chuckled. "For now." She helped him carry food from the kitchen into the dining room. "Why do you suppose Uncle Dominic went to such extremes to ensure Lazz and Ariana married? I mean, creating a marriage contract seems a bit out there. He couldn't be certain they were experiencing an early form of The Inferno. After all, they were only children."

Constantine shrugged. "Apparently Dominic decided that marrying someone who wasn't his Inferno bride guaranteed a disastrous marriage and he didn't want Lazz and Ariana to experience what he did with his wife, Laura."

Gianna stiffened. "No, that's not right. You or your father must have misunderstood."

He shook his head. "I don't think so. Weren't your aunt and uncle planning to divorce shortly before their deaths?"

"Yes, but the two definitely felt The Inferno for each other. Even though they were Inferno soul mates, it didn't work out for them." She set the plates on the table, avoiding his gaze. "That's what I've been trying to explain to you. Experiencing The Inferno isn't a guarantee of a happy marriage. That's why I want to make sure we're compatible before we take our relationship any further."

"Che cavolo!" He snagged her chin, forcing her to look at him, practically vibrating with fury. "Are you telling me

you've inflicted me with The Inferno, *but we may never know true happiness together?*"

Misery invaded her gaze. "Yes. That's exactly what I'm saying."

Seven

Gianna winced at the combination of outrage and anger that burned in Constantine's expression.

"Why would you do this to us?" he demanded in Italian.

She allowed a hint of her own temper to show. "You keep saying that like I had a choice. I didn't and I don't. It just happens, okay? The Inferno chooses, not me."

"That is a very convenient gift," he accused. "All you have to say to escape blame is it's not your fault. It's The Inferno."

"It *isn't* my fault. And it *was* The Inferno." She confronted him, hands on her hips. "Do you really think I took one look at you in all your magnificence and decided… Yeah, let's zap him for the rest of our lives?"

"I don't know." He stuck his truly magnificent nose in her face, speaking between gritted teeth. "Did you?"

She wanted to scream in frustration. "We were meeting

for the first time when it happened! Until then, we'd never spoken one word to each other. Why would I want to saddle myself with a man I don't even know?" She held up her hand before he could offer another sarcastic comment. "Don't you get it? The Inferno works the way it works. I'm as much a victim of it as you are. Do you think I like having decisions made for me? That I like having some weird flash of heat and electricity decide that you're the one?"

"Considering you would have chosen d'Angelo over me, maybe you're better off trusting The Inferno," he shot back.

"Oh! That is beyond low—"

He cut her off without hesitation, all the while struggling to rein in his temper. "Let me see if I have this straight. You and I have felt The Inferno."

She folded her arms across her chest and glared. "Yes."

"But someday you may shake another man's hand and feel The Inferno for him." Constantine had keyed in on the one part of this entire situation that she hated the most. "I will only want you and no other woman for the rest of my days. You may Inferno any number of men. Is that correct?"

Her cheeks warmed and she nodded. "I think so, yes."

Until this moment she hadn't realized how much he resented The Inferno or what had happened between them. Of course, she'd grown up with The Inferno, he hadn't. She'd heard Primo and Nonna relate the "fairy tale" of their first meeting from the time she was a toddler, had seen the joy and happiness between her own parents, just as she'd witnessed the misery Uncle Dominic and Aunt Laura had been unable to conceal. It made for a confusing picture.

Her cousins and brothers had never believed in the family "blessing" or "curse" as they'd jokingly called it. They'd held tight to their lack of faith right up until it had happened to them. Throughout it all, Gianna had stood on the sidelines watching while, one by one, cousin and brother had fallen and fallen hard. And she'd kept her mouth firmly shut about what she'd learned on her thirteenth birthday, not wanting to put a damper on all that delirious "forever after" Inferno love.

If they only knew.

The years had passed and she'd waited to see whether a female Dante was capable of feeling The Inferno, of sharing it with her chosen mate, not quite sure whether or not she wanted the experience. Then it happened. What she hadn't foreseen was Constantine's adverse reaction. Her indignation faded.

"You hate The Inferno, don't you?" she asked miserably.

"I hate that it's taken away my choice," Constantine admitted. He corralled the intensity of his anger. "That it eats into my self-control and ability to determine my own destiny. That I am unable to decide yes, no or maybe, and am simply swept along like a helpless minnow plummeting over the rapids of a raging river."

Gianna struggled to conceal her pain. All this time she'd thought he'd wanted her. And all this time he'd resented that want. The knowledge forced her to offer a way out. It was the only honorable course available to her. She took a step back so her closeness wouldn't influence him. Ridiculous, really. If they'd felt the unrelenting pull when they'd been separated by six thousand miles of land and ocean, a few feet wasn't going to change anything.

"Would you rather not feel The Inferno?" she forced herself to ask. "If I could undo it, take it away, would you want me to?"

Instead of jumping at the offer, to her surprise and relief he hesitated. "You can do this?"

"I don't know," she admitted. "I've never tried."

"If you did, I would feel nothing for you?"

She shook her head, unable to give him an honest answer. "I have no idea. It's possible."

He stared down at his palm for several long minutes, digging his thumb into the center while he considered. "It's hard for me to imagine not wanting you." He focused on her once again. "What about you? If you took back The Inferno would you still feel it toward me?"

She bit down on her lip to keep it from trembling. "I think I'll no longer feel it for you when I feel it for someone else. *If* I feel it for someone else." Tears flooded her eyes and she blinked them away. She flat-out dreaded the day that would happen. She couldn't even imagine loving someone more than Constantine. "All I know for certain is that I've never wanted anyone but you or felt The Inferno with any other man than you. Even so, I can't make any promises for the future."

He softened ever so slightly. "But then, that's life, isn't it? People fall in love and marry. For some it lasts a lifetime. For others..." He shrugged. "Not so long."

Now for the tough question. "Do we keep going and see if it'll work for us?" Her throat thickened and she had to force the words out. "Or do we put a stop to it while we still can?"

The question hung between them for a timeless moment. Then, "I can't," Constantine said. Just those two harsh words, sounding as though they'd been ripped from the deepest part of him. For an instant, her world ended until he added, "I can't let you go."

She moved without conscious thought, hurling herself into his arms. "Oh, Constantine."

He lifted her face to his and kissed her. Deep. Urgent. Desperate kisses. Taking her under until nothing existed but him. His mouth. His touch. The relentless burn of The Inferno. She suspected they'd have taken that final, irrevocable step if her stomach hadn't chosen that moment to growl. She broke away with a laugh, one he shared.

He tucked a lock of hair he'd loosened during their embrace behind her ear. "Okay, *piccola*. Here's what we'll do. We'll spend the next month keeping our promise to Primo. We'll get to know each other. Then we'll decide about The Inferno."

She could scarcely contain her relief. She'd been so afraid he'd want to be released from the hold of The Inferno, despite the intense desire they shared. It said a lot that neither of them questioned the level of passion they felt for the other. At least that aspect of their relationship had never been in doubt.

If they managed to put an end to The Inferno, the fragile bud of trust developing between them would be nipped off. The slow growth of passion into something deeper and more permanent would be cut down before it had a chance to bloom. By moving forward that tiny bud would have the opportunity to flourish and she realized just how badly she wanted to see what sort of flower blossomed as a result. She had a feeling it would be spectacular beyond belief.

A smile exploded from her, wide and radiant. "Well, okay. That's what we'll do. We'll get to know each other better." She gestured toward the table with trembling hands and scolded, "What are you waiting for? Sit and eat. Breakfast is getting cold."

The next two weeks flew by. Gianna and Constantine approached the whole "getting to know each other" agreement a trifle self-consciously. At least, that was how she felt about their initial dates, dates to dinner or the movies or a quiet evening at home.

Granted, once they were together for a short time, the awkwardness vanished. In its place passion exploded, a passion they struggled to contain. She wished she could say nothing more than sheer lust existed between them, but that would be a lie, Gianna conceded. The truth was, she *liked* Constantine.

She enjoyed his intellect, and his observations about life. She found his work fascinating, particularly the interior design branch of Romano Restoration since she utilized similar skills and abilities when planning an event or staging one of Dantes' high-end receptions. Constantine also possessed a calmness she appreciated and a way of taking control of a situation by smoothing over any rough edges. And as much as she'd like to fault him for holding her at a firm distance, she couldn't fault his sense of honor, not when it went to the very core of who he was as a man.

Sitting behind her desk, Gianna tapped a pen against the catering contract spread across the glass tabletop while she analyzed her relationship with Constantine. She didn't even mind that he tended to be a bit of a control freak. Even there, they meshed well. She might be a bit scattered at times and possess a strong tendency to act on impulse, particularly in her personal life—David being a prime example. But when it came to her job, she was detail-oriented and on top of things. Her work at Dantes demanded it.

The phone at her elbow rang and she answered it absently, perking up when Constantine's sexy accent sounded in her ear. "How is your day going, *piccola?*" he asked.

Mmm. Just hearing his voice made her want to melt right into her chair. "Better now that you've called," she admitted.

"Then I'm sorry to say that I'm about to make your day worse."

"Tonight?" she guessed with a disappointed sigh.

A light tap sounded at her door and Juice, a longtime family friend, stuck his gleaming bald head into her office. He'd first been adopted by the Dantes when he'd worked for her brother's private security firm, before Luc had taken over Dantes Courier Service. Juice specialized in background checks, finding what others didn't want found, and all things stored in cyberspace. Occasionally he helped the Dantes with his expertise. Gianna was hoping this would be one of those times. She waved him in and toward a seat near her desk.

"Do you need to change our plans?" she asked Constantine.

"I have to cancel them, I'm afraid. Some last minute alterations to a proposal."

"Oh, no," she said sympathetically. "Not the Diamondt account, I hope."

"I'm afraid so."

"But, you've worked so hard on that one. And the plans you've designed for the restoration are gorgeous. What's the problem?"

"A family disagreement. Apparently there's a son-in-law who owns enough of his late wife's share of the family business that they need his approval on my restoration project before going to contract."

"It would have helped if they'd told you about him beforehand."

"My thoughts, exactly. Now I am forced to make a number of alterations that I hope will satisfy all the various parties. I may even have to fly up there to meet with Moretti in order to resolve the problem."

"Moretti? Is that the son-in-law's name?" For some reason it rang a distant, rather muffled, bell. "Sounds like the Diamondts and the Dantes have something in common. We both have our little family squabbles that require a firm hand to resolve. In our case, Primo's hand."

"Not even close," he assured her. "The Dantes adore each other and squabble accordingly. The Diamondts put me more in mind of the Borgias. Unfortunately they don't have a Primo to straighten them out, which means they're all jockeying for control."

She chuckled. "That bad, huh? Okay, I'll let you get back to it. How about tomorrow? Do you have to work over the weekend?"

"I'm free both days," he assured her. "Think about how you'd like to spend them."

"I'll do that." She spared Juice a quick glance and kept her voice light and casual. "I'll talk to you later."

A brief pause, then, "You're not alone, are you?"

"Good guess."

"Family?"

She winked at Juice to include him in the conversation. "An old family friend."

"You tempt me to say something that will make you blush."

"Do that and it will be the topic of conversation for quite some time to come," she warned.

"Ah." It took every ounce of self-possession to keep from shuddering at the deep, sexy way he drew out the sound. "That sort of old family friend. I assume that means you're not the only *chiacchierona*."

"He'd resent that. He'd also resemble it—but only on occasion. In his line of work he has to know when to talk… and when not to."

That elicited a laugh. "Then I'll spare your blushes and call later when we can talk dirty in private."

He'd succeeded in making her blush, anyway, a fact Juice noted with an uplifted eyebrow. "I'll definitely make it worth your while," she shot back.

"Now I'm blushing."

And with that the line went dead, leaving her grinning like an idiot.

"I see the rumors aren't rumors, after all," Juice observed in a deep, rumbling bass. "Would I be correct in assuming Constantine Romano caused you to turn that interesting shade of red?"

Her smile broadened. "You would."

"Serious?"

She hesitated, then nodded. "I think so."

"I'm happy for you." He leaned forward and rested his massive arms on his knees. "So what's up, G? You said you had a job for me."

"I do." She glanced toward the open door. Better if they weren't overheard, she decided, and crossed her office to close it. "Would it be possible to keep this between the two of us?" she asked, resuming her seat.

"I'd have to know the particulars before I answered that question."

She blew out a sigh. "Fair enough. I'd like you to find a diamond for me. It went missing about a year and a half ago."

"I don't suppose you're talking about Brimstone?"

Her mouth dropped open. "You *know* about Brimstone?"

"I know lots of stuff." His dark eyes gleamed with laughter. "Most of which you don't."

"That doesn't seem fair," she complained. "I don't suppose you can tell me the whereabouts of Brimstone?"

"I can't."

Hmm. "Can't…or won't?"

"Can't," he repeated gently. "I don't know where it is."

"Could you find out?"

His gaze intensified. No wonder Luc had hired Juice. Brilliant. Able to find anything or anyone. And, when he chose to be, one of the most intimidating men she'd ever met. "Why do you want to find it?"

"Someone else is after the stone and I think the Dantes should find it first."

"Makes sense."

"One more thing… In addition to finding Brimstone, there's a person I want you to track down. Don't approach him or do anything once you locate him," she hastened to add. "Just keep tabs on him."

"If you're talking about David d'Angelo, that's already covered."

She should have known. "Luc?" she guessed.

He ticked off on his fingers. "Luc. Rafe. Draco. Your father. Primo. Various cousins. Pretty much the whole Dante clan."

Alarm filled her. "What are they going to do when you find him?"

"Make him disappear." He paused a beat. Then a slow grin split his dark face. "God, you're easy. I'm kidding, G. They want the same thing you do. To keep tabs on the guy. Dig up any dirt on him. Make sure he doesn't take advantage of some other poor woman. They want to see him pay…legally. After what he did to you, would you expect any less?"

"Oh." For a minute there, she'd actually believed him about making David disappear. Scary thought. She cleared her throat. "Well, okay, then."

"I'll see what I can do about Brimstone. Anything else?"

"That's it." She eyed him in open curiosity. "What do you think the chances are you'll find it?"

"Fair-to-middlin'. What do you think the chances are that you and Constantine will hook up?"

"We're only dating, Juice."

He tipped his head to one side. "I heard engaged."

"Nope. Just dating."

"Okay." He stood and headed for the door, turning at the last moment. "Just so you know, I have a hundred on this weekend."

She stared in confusion. "Excuse me?"

"The pool for when you and Constantine will make it official. I have this weekend. Winning might upgrade the chances of my finding Brimstone from fair-to-middling to who's-your-daddy." And with that, he exited her office.

It took Gianna a full thirty seconds to catch her breath sufficiently to respond. When she did, she bellowed, *"Rafe!"*

Taking pity on Constantine and his business woes, Gianna decided to pick up dinner and drop it off at Romano Restoration. She wouldn't stay, she promised herself. If he could spare a half hour she'd let him talk her into hanging around long enough to share a meal with him. But otherwise she'd make herself scarce so he could put the finishing touches on his proposal.

She caught a cab to his office building. The receptionist was no longer on duty, but the security guard tipped his cap when he saw her, recognizing her from her frequent visits. He even called the elevator for her, holding the door with a friendly smile. She stepped inside and used the key Constantine had given her to access his apartment. All the while, the delicious scent of the dinner she'd picked up at the Oriental Pearl filled the small space.

He wasn't in the apartment, which meant she'd find him in his office. She'd assumed as much, but she had a few things she wanted to nab before she joined him. Snagging a throw off the back of his couch, she gathered up napkins, a bottle of wine and wineglasses. At the last minute she remembered to add a bottle opener to her stash and headed downstairs. Sure enough, he sat behind his desk, hard at work.

She paused unnoticed in the doorway and took the opportunity to study him. Usually he sensed her. But she suspected he was so focused on the job at hand that it would take more than even The Inferno to pry him loose.

His ink-black hair fell across his forehead in thick, unruly waves. She'd have called them curls, but suspected he'd take immediate exception to the term, a fact that made her smile. He jotted a note in the margin of the paper he held, the desk lamp casting sharp light across his features.

Dear heaven, but he was a gorgeous man. Elegant, and yet intensely male. His features were also intensely male—a firm, straight nose, a wide sensuous mouth, strong chin and jaw, high, aristocratic cheekbones. But the most devastating feature of all were his eyes. So dark. So sharp. So direct and honest.

Something deep inside of her gave a quick tug. A little lurch. She closed her eyes, unable to hide from the truth. She suspected that if she didn't actually love this man, she was teetering on the brink. Dante pride had kept her from admitting it, but she couldn't lie to herself. Not now. She'd fallen in lust the moment they'd touched. Her family called it The Inferno, but she knew lust when she felt it.

At some point in the dozen plus days they'd been together,

her feelings for him had grown. Deepened. Matured. It would only take a tiny nudge to send her tumbling. She almost laughed at the thought. If left to Constantine, it wouldn't be a nudge, but a full-body tackle from "maybe" to "happily ever after."

She knew the instant he sensed her. A predatory stillness consumed him. He didn't move. Didn't speak. He simply lifted his eyes and stared at her. She returned the look, not moving or speaking, either. She let him eat her alive with his gaze while she returned the favor.

"Are you real?" he asked with a slow smile. "Or just a delicious dream?"

"Definitely real." She held up the bag of food. "And extra delicious. Can you spare a few minutes for dinner?"

His smile grew. "Maybe you can feed me while I work."

"Now you are dreaming."

He chuckled. "It was worth a try." He eyed the blanket she carried. "Cold?"

"Nope. I thought we'd have a picnic." She slipped out of her heels. "Kick off your shoes and relax for a few minutes."

He hesitated, shook his head. "I don't kick off my shoes."

That gave her pause. "Seriously? Never?"

"Seriously. Never." His expression darkened. "You can't be ready to go at a moment's notice if you're not wearing your shoes."

She blinked. That never would have occurred to her. "I'm not sure what might happen in the next half hour that you'll need to be ready to go at a moment's notice, but I'll take your word for it."

"Thanks."

Now she knew something was off. Thinking back she realized that even when she and Constantine had been their most relaxed during evenings at her row house, he'd never taken off his shoes. He'd also kept his possessions neatly gathered so all he had to do was pick them up on his way out the door.

Not the least like her. Half her possessions were scattered across every Dante home in the Bay Area. The Italian version of *mi casa es su casa*. She'd have dismissed Constantine's obsessiveness as a personality quirk if she hadn't caught that telltale darkness flitting across the hard contours of his face. Something was up there and she made a mental note to explore it at a future date. Until then, no point in making a big deal about it or attempting to involve him in a heavy discussion. Not when he was in the middle of a work crisis.

Keeping the mood light and easy, Gianna offered a cheerful smile and shrugged. "Oh. Okay. Keep your shoes on if it makes you more comfortable." She held up the bag of goodies. "Hungry?"

"What did you bring for us?" he asked, only too happy to go along with the change of subject.

She grinned. "Everything."

The next half hour turned out to be a brief moment of enchantment. They spent the time together eating and laughing, using the chopsticks that came with their meal to feed each other tidbits from the selection of cartons. The office setting faded into the background while they sat on the butter-soft blanket she'd liberated from his apartment. The light from his desk barely reached them, illuminating their impromptu picnic with a muted, distant glow.

"Will it always be like this?" she asked at one point while she refilled their wineglasses.

He paused, chopsticks lifted halfway to her mouth. "Like what?"

"Fun. Romantic." She shrugged. "Wonderful."

Raw pleasure shot through his gaze. "Considering who I have to be fun, romantic and wonderful with, it shouldn't be too difficult," he replied, much to her delight. "Have you thought about what you'd like to do this weekend?"

She hesitated. "There's one thing…"

"Name it."

"My family owns a place about three hours north of here. It's on a good-size lake. Great fishing and sailing. Over the years we've acquired all the property around it, so it's pretty private. Maybe Ariana mentioned it to you?" she asked uncertainly. "The entire family goes each summer for a huge Dante blowout."

"Sounds like fun. Is this weekend the family blow-out?"

"No, not for another few weeks." She hesitated. "I thought we could go ahead of time, just for the weekend."

"I'm not sure this is what Primo had in mind when he gave us a month to get to know each other better."

"True." She caught her lip between her teeth. "Even so, I'd like to go."

He studied her for a moment and she wondered if he could read the truth in her face, if he could tell she had an ulterior motive. "If that's what you'd like, of course we can go to the lake. Do we need permission from Primo?"

She shook her head. "My brothers and cousins and I all have carte blanche to visit anytime we want. We can either stay at the main house or in one of the cabins by the lake. You can decide which you prefer when we get there."

"What's going on, Gianna?" he asked bluntly.

She drew her legs close to her chest and wrapped her arms around them, resting her chin on her knees. All the while she avoided his gaze. "I'd just like to take you to the lake without my entire family watching our every move."

"And…?"

She blew out a sigh, deciding to come clean. "And, I'd like you to help me get over my fear of the water without my relatives catching on."

He sat up straight. "*Accidenti!* Of course I'll help you if I can. But I'm not qualified to handle something so serious." He reached for her, unwrapping her arms and legs, and tucked her tight against him. The firm beat of his heart steadied her as nothing else could have. "What has caused this fear, do you remember?"

She leaned into him. "It started when Uncle Dominic and Aunt Laura drowned. I was terrified to go in the water after that."

He considered that for a moment. "They drowned while sailing, yes? It didn't occur at the lake?"

She shook her head. "I'd never have been able to return to the lake if it had happened there."

His frown deepened. "Why hasn't your family helped you get over this fear?"

"They don't know," she confessed. "I've kept it hidden all these years. I sunbathe and splash a bit in the shallows. But I spend my time there hiking or reading or any activity that doesn't involve swimming." She searched his face. "Would you be willing to try to help me?"

"For you? Anything."

She made a sound, half laugh, half sigh. "I'm not sure whether to be grateful or sorry."

He lifted her face to his. "I vote for grateful." He feathered a kiss across her mouth. "Very grateful."

As it turned out, Constantine didn't return to work until a long time later.

* * *

Constantine picked up Gianna early the next morning. One look at her face warned she hadn't slept well. He took her overnight bag and tucked it away in the trunk of his Porsche.

"We don't need to do this, you know," he informed her as they headed out of the city. "You're allowed to change your mind."

She hid her exhaustion behind a pair of sunglasses, but the set of her chin told its own story. She'd go through with her plan no matter how difficult. "You can thank David for this," she told him.

He spared her a brief, hard look. "Explain."

"He scared me. Terrified me. As a result, I discovered something about myself." She looked at him then, glaring over the top of her sunglasses. "I don't like being afraid."

"I'll protect you from d'Angelo. I swear it."

To his intense pleasure, she nodded in complete agreement. "Of course you will. Because that's who you are. But here's the thing…" She angled her body in his direction and stabbed her finger to emphasize her point. "Even though I was terrified, I still found a way to escape."

He allowed his admiration to show. "Yes, you did."

"If I can overcome my fear of David, I can overcome my fear of the water. And that's what I'm going to do." She nudged her sunglasses higher on the bridge of her nose in a decisive movement. "With your help, that is."

He shot her a swift grin. "I've thought of a possible solution."

"Oh, yeah? What's that?"

"I'll distract you."

"Hmm. Not sure that'll work. I don't think there's anything you can do that'll distract me to that extent."

"Sure it will."

"What?"

"Two words… Skinny. Dipping."

She chuckled, relaxing for the first time that morning. "Okay, that just might work."

He could tell she thought he was kidding. In just a little over two hours she'd find out he was serious. He smiled in anticipation.

Very, very serious.

Eight

They arrived at the Dantes' summer property right at noon. Constantine parked in a gravel section between a large workshop and equally generous-size storage shed. He took a moment to stretch, then looked around in appreciation.

"Impressive," he said to Gianna. "And quite beautiful. Peaceful."

She smiled, clearly pleased with his reaction. "We like it."

The main residence, a rambling rough-hewn log building, complete with a pair of stone chimneys, perched on the lake's edge. Two more modern wings bookended the main section and cantilevered over the water. On the lakefront, a pier and boathouse occupied one end of the curved shoreline and the Dantes had trucked in soft white sand to form a sweeping beach. Tucked into the nearby woods he spotted individual cabins.

Gianna noticed the direction of his gaze and gestured

toward the closest one. "For the married couples who prefer a bit more privacy than being under one roof with everyone else."

"And if the couple in question isn't married?"

She shot him an impish grin and jerked her head toward the main house. "Opposite wings."

"And of those two options, where would you prefer to spend the night?"

Her eyes narrowed in consideration and she caught her lower lip between her teeth. For some reason she was having trouble making a decision. "The first cabin," she finally decided. "That way we don't have to open up the main house. Plus the closest cabin has two bedrooms."

"Are we going to use both?"

She fussed with her sunglasses for a moment. "What happens if we only use one?" she asked. She tried to make the question sound casual and failed miserably.

"You and I announce our engagement the moment we return," he answered, not the least casual about his response.

"Okay," she said. Reaching inside the car, she snagged the groceries they'd picked up and started across the driveway toward the cabin.

Okay? What did she mean by that? "Okay, we can announce our engagement?" he called after her. "Or, okay we'll use separate bedrooms?"

"Yes," she tossed over her shoulder.

He snatched up their bags with a broad grin and followed after her, appreciating the view. Her endless legs ate up the distance with ease, the feminine sway of her pert backside drawing his gaze. Her hair tumbled down her back in loose curls, the sunlight losing itself in the glorious streaks of brown and gold. What would she say if she knew he'd purchased a Dantes' Eternity engagement ring…just in case? Panic, or set the fastest wedding date on record?

Maybe he'd find out.

After grabbing a quick lunch, Gianna took Constantine on a tour of the complex, followed by a hike partway around the huge lake. He knew she was avoiding the true purpose for their visit. But he didn't push, instead allowing her to set the pace. She'd tell him when she was ready to act.

They returned to the cabin late that afternoon to enjoy a cup of coffee on the deck and Constantine leaned back in his chair, stacking his feet on the top railing. The cabin rested within the protective embrace of a stand of cedar trees, about fifty feet from the water. A solid two hundred yards from shore a raft teetered back and forth against the slap and drag of gentle wind-driven waves. From his current position he could look out across the shimmering blue lake to the dense forest beyond, with the Sierra Nevada mountains rising majestically in the background. It was an amazing sight, one he'd be all too happy to view on a regular basis. No wonder the Dantes loved this place. And how fortunate to have been able to acquire all the surrounding property. He couldn't help but wonder how many years that had taken.

"It's getting late," Gianna commented.

Constantine kept his voice calm and nonchalant. "The sun doesn't set for hours yet."

"Still…" She took a final swallow of coffee and set her mug onto the glass-topped table beside her with a decisive click. "Let's get this over with."

Without another word, she stood and disappeared inside the cabin. He followed in time to see her vanish into the bedroom she'd staked out, and continued on to his own. Stripping off his clothes, he changed into trunks and returned to the deck.

Gianna joined him a few minutes later, wearing a pale

lime-green one-piece, the color somehow intensifying the unusual shade of her eyes. The squared bodice was modest, just hinting at her generous cleavage. And she'd tied a misty drape at her waist that fell to her calves in a swirl of blues and greens. All he could think about was how quickly he could strip away that drape, followed by her swimsuit.

She shot him a questioning glance over her shoulder. "What?"

He gave her a slow, hungry smile. "Skinny. Dipping."

She darted across the deck with a laugh, her curls bouncing against her back. "You have to catch me first."

A short stack of steps ended at a narrow pathway leading to the stretch of beach closest to the dock and boathouse. She hurdled over the stairs in a practiced maneuver and hit the path at a dead run. The predator in him roared to life and he gave chase. He would have caught her, too, if she hadn't frozen at the water's edge. Her stillness had him pulling up beside her, careful not to do anything that might spook her.

"You don't have to go in," he reassured.

"I know, but I've delayed long enough," she said grimly. She untied the drape and tossed it onto the sand in a resolute manner. "Let's give it a try and see what happens."

It didn't take long. Constantine stuck right by Gianna's side. She waded in until the water lapped around her waist. One minute she seemed perfectly normal and the next minute her breath hitched and she spun awkwardly around. Before he could sweep her from the water to safety, she tripped, plummeting beneath the surface.

He was on her within seconds, snatching her up and lifting her high in his arms. But the damage had been done. She lost it. Curling into him, she choked on the water she'd swallowed, weeping in terror. He carried her straight to the cabin and into the bathroom. He turned on the shower, the spray hard and hot. With her still in his arms, he walked into the huge mosaic tiled stall.

"I'm okay, I'm okay," she wept.

"I know you are. We'll just stand here, anyway, until you're more okay."

He lowered her onto her feet and pushed the wet hair from her eyes and simply held her tight against his chest until her shuddering sobs faded and her heartbeat calmed to a slower rate. The heat helped loosen her tight muscles and ease her trembling. Finally she tilted her head back and looked at him.

"Damn," she whispered.

His mouth twitched. "Didn't go the way you planned?" he asked tenderly.

She slicked the moisture from her face. "You could say that."

"Did you really expect your phobia would disappear the minute you stepped in the water?"

"Yes," she grumbled. "I did. It's an irrational knee-jerk reaction. I'm not the one who drowned."

"Clearly."

"I've never even had a close call," she continued. "There's no logical reason for me to fear the water."

He hated to suggest it, but given the circumstances… "Have you considered therapy?"

"No. It wasn't until David that I was even willing to accept that I had a problem." She reached around him to turn off the water and squeezed the water from her hair. "I want you to know this is unacceptable."

"The shower?"

"No." A brief smile flirted with her mouth. "That was sort of nice."

"I can turn the water back on and we can have some more nice," he offered generously.

Her smile grew. "Thanks, but no." She exited the stall and grabbed a towel for herself and tossed him the spare. She dried herself in short, angry movements. "I'm telling you, Constantine, before we leave here I *will* get over this fear. When David had me trapped in his car, I refused to allow him to scare me so badly I couldn't act. I'm not going to let some ridiculous phobia keep me from enjoying the lake now."

Constantine dried himself at a more leisurely pace. "I don't doubt it. Not if you've made up your mind to do it."

She nodded decisively. "Darned right. I used to love to swim. I used to spend all day out on the raft and do flips and dives off of it." She tossed her towel onto the floor. "I was good, damn it."

"Ready to go again or do you want to wait until morning?"

Gianna vacillated for a split second. He saw the instant she came to a decision, her mouth assuming a stubborn slant. "No. Now. Right this second while I'm still mad. Before I remember to be scared again."

She practically ran from the bathroom. He went after her, determined to keep pace with her every step of the way. This time he'd be ready. This time she wouldn't go under.

The instant they hit sand, he took her hand in his. Farther out in the lake the wooden raft rocked, creaking and jangling against its metal chain and anchor. Together they walked to the water's edge where he tugged her to a standstill. "Not so deep this time," he instructed. "And not so fast."

She nodded in agreement. Taking a deep breath, she waded in until the water hit her knees. Then she slowly stooped, allowing the water to wash upward over her body. He followed her down. Her fingers tightened in his and her breathing kicked up a notch.

Screwing her eyes closed, she muttered, "Just like a

bath." She settled onto the lake bottom, the water lapping around her chest. "That's all I'm doing. Soaking in a nice deep bathtub."

Constantine plastered himself behind her and wrapped his arms around her waist. He drew her back between his legs and pressed her rigid spine tight against his chest. "I'm thinking either Hawaii or Alaska."

Gianna jerked in surprise at the non sequitur. "What?"

"For our honeymoon. Follow my reasoning here… Alaska requires a lot of clothes because even in the summer it can be chilly. But you have that unbelievable scenery and a lot of nakedness in front of a roaring fire."

"Have you lost your mind?" She splashed water in his direction. "We're not even engaged."

"The benefits of Hawaii are the lack of clothes…so, more nakedness."

"I'm beginning to sense a theme here," she said drily.

"Well, it is our honeymoon. Nakedness will be involved."

She held up her left hand and shook it in his face. "Please note. Bare finger. Bare finger equals no engagement. No engagement equals no honeymoon."

Hmm. True. But had she noticed she wasn't panicking? Might be too soon to point out that minor detail. He allowed his hand to drift upward from her waist to settle just beneath her breasts. Maybe it was the buoyancy of the water that caused his thumb to drift upward, as well. Or maybe he'd lost control over it and it went crazy all on its own. Somehow it swept across her breast. Repeatedly.

"We could always start with the honeymoon," he suggested. "Get that out of the way first. Work on the engagement and wedding afterward."

She shivered. "Honor and all that, remember?"

She sounded a bit desperate, as though she were reminding herself as well as him. The possibility made him grin. "Parts of me remember. Other parts…" he shook his head "I am forced to admit, not so much."

"Maybe you should send a memo to those other parts."

Taking a chance, he scooped her up and spun her around to face him. Her legs closed automatically around his waist. At the same time, her arms wrapped tight around his neck. She gazed into his eyes, a funny little smile catching at the corners of her mouth.

"You don't think I know what you're doing, but I do," she informed him.

"And what am I doing?"

"Distracting me." She tilted her head to one side. "What do you say I distract you instead?"

He didn't have an opportunity to respond. She took his mouth in a deep, hungry kiss. Her lips parted, beckoning him inward. He didn't need a second invitation. He sank into honeyed warmth, their tongues dueling briefly, mating slowly, pleasuring thoroughly.

Using extreme care, he eased them into deeper water, keeping her tight within his control. Then he slid one hand downward over her abdomen to the top of her leg where silky bathing suit met satiny skin. He drew a finger along the elastic edge, then slipped under.

Gianna buried her face against Constantine's shoulder and released a sound that threatened his sanity. A helpless feminine plea. A soft siren's call that spoke of blatant need. He had no choice but to respond, to try to give her what she desired. He found the hot core of her and stroked. She came apart in his arms, her sweet cry drifting across the lake.

It took her a long moment to recover her voice enough to speak. "I can't stand it any longer, Constantine," she managed to say.

"Neither can I."

More than anything he wanted to keep his promise and not touch her until his ring was on her finger or they were married. But he'd reached the end of his rope. He couldn't keep his hands off her a minute longer. Cradling her close, he waded toward shore.

Before the sun set, Constantine intended to make Gianna his in every sense of the word.

Constantine carried Gianna to the cabin with a strength and ease that impacted on the most feminine level. He kicked open the door to her bedroom and entered. The tantalizing scent of forest cedar gently spiced the air. It was dusky and cool, lit only by the late-afternoon sunlight filtering through the gauzy drapes covering the windows. The fading light slid into the room, bathing the bed in a benevolent rosy glow.

He set her on her feet and took a step back. She understood why. He wanted her to be certain, to commit without his touch influencing her. What he didn't understand was that he was the only man with whom she could commit. For the next few hours she intended to forget everything but the two of them. With the rays of a setting sun cloaking them and the privacy of their mountain retreat to hide them away from prying eyes, this moment would be theirs. Just one special day to come together without worrying about right or wrong, or The Inferno, or family expectations.

Constantine continued to keep his distance. "Are you sure, Gianna?"

"Oh, yes. Definitely, yes."

Even though she knew they both wanted this more than anything else, she caught something in his expression, just a brief flash that hinted at regret. It didn't take any guesswork to figure out the cause. She closed the distance between them, leaned into him and sighed in relief the instant his arms closed tight around her. It was time. Time to let go of her pride and follow her heart.

Long past time.

"As much as I'd like to make love to you, Constantine, we can't take this any further," she informed him. She pulled back and smoothed the furrow lining his brow with a tender hand. "Not quite yet. I believe there's something you have to do first so that tonight is the way it should be. The way we'll always want to remember it. A night without regrets or blemish."

A slow smile built across his face, the most beautiful smile she'd ever seen. Ever so gently, he swept the back of his hand across her cheek. "Thank you for this," he whispered.

"Anytime," she whispered back.

He took her hands in his and dropped to one knee. If anyone else had done such a thing, it would have been beyond corny. In this special moment, it was beyond romantic. "Gianna Marie Fiorella Dante, will you do me the honor of becoming my wife?"

She opened her heart, allowing it to show in every bit of her expression. "Yes, Constantine. I'll marry you."

He stood, cupping her face. "No second thoughts?"

Her tearful smile felt shaky, but from happiness not nervousness. "Not a single one. I couldn't have chosen a more perfect man to share a more perfect moment."

The contours of his face softened, hunger kicking in. "I don't know if I can make this perfect for you, but I swear I'll do my best."

Constantine kissed her with unmistakable passion, stamping her with his possession in the most delicious way. It went beyond mere exploration, and became a thorough taking. Not rushed. But slow and deep and giving.

Gianna's breathing quickened, desire rising like a storm-driven tide, building inexorably, need an immense tidal wave flinging itself toward shore. It broke, spilling over her in a great rush and she clung to him, hanging on tight, then tighter. His tongue dueled with hers, lips and mouth teasing, mating, and he thrust his hands deep into her hair, using the tangle of thick heavy curls to anchor her to him.

"Finally," he muttered. "Your hair has been driving me crazy all day. Flirting. Taunting. But not anymore." He wrapped the weighty mass around his hand and drew her up. "Now you can't get away."

Her mouth curved into a slow smile. "Why would I want to get away? There's only one place I want to be and that's in bed with you."

He said something in Italian. Something thick and dark and demanding. For some reason, she couldn't make sense of it. "Take off your swimsuit," he repeated in English.

She lifted her chin in open challenge. "Take it off me."

His gaze flared darkly. "My pleasure."

His fingers slid from her hair to the narrow straps banding her shoulders. He lowered them, sweeping them down her arms inch by excruciating inch. A light breeze drifted in through the open window and tripped along her spine. Her suit slipped downward, settling around her hips. A swift, gentle tug and it slid to her ankles.

She stepped free of her suit and stood nude before him in acres of skin turned blush-pink beneath the benevolent kiss of a ruby sun. She thought she'd feel nervous or apprehensive or self-conscious. Instead she just felt the rightness of being with him.

"Your turn," she informed him.

He couldn't take his eyes off her. "I'm a little busy." He cupped her breast and stroked the tip with the rough pad of his thumb. "I've never seen anything so beautiful."

Her nipple tightened in response and she shuddered, the

intense pleasure arrowing straight to her core, making her painfully aware of her femininity. She burned with it, a melting heat that made her want to dissolve into his arms.

She shook her head to clear the sensual fog. "There's this interesting rumor going around that what you have in mind can't be accomplished unless you're naked, too." She shot him a teasing smile. "Besides, it's only fair."

"Normally I'd say you shouldn't listen to rumors." His voice deepened. "Though in this case, there may be some truth to them."

His fingers dragged across the peak of her breast again, the sensation a delicious agony, and she lost it. With a muffled cry of demand, she yanked him to her, kissing every inch of him she could reach. Touching every bit of him. The endless width of his chest. The ripple of hard, curving muscle and toned sinew. The rumble strips down his abdomen. An endless, beautiful display of burning hot skin. And it was all hers.

God, he was in incredible shape, especially for a man who spent his life in an office. Or maybe he didn't. Maybe he helped out with the actual restoration process. Something had put all those delicious ridges of muscle on his chest and shoulders.

Unable to help herself, she pressed a kiss just above his heart. He groaned softly and caught her close. "You undo me, *piccola,*" he whispered. She reached for his swim trunks and he stopped her. "Considering my current state, I think I'd better take care of this part myself."

In one swift move, he stripped off the trunks. He was painfully heavy with desire and she shivered before the intense maleness of him. As though sensing her skittishness, he corralled her in the direction of the bed, tossing aside the covers. She tumbled backward onto the thick, soft mattress, the cotton sheet like velvet against her back. He braced himself above her, hovering for an endless moment. Inch by inch, he lowered himself onto her, pressing her into softness while covering her with delicious heat.

"Constantine!" His name escaped in a pleading sigh, asking for something she couldn't quite bring herself to express in any other way. She couldn't get enough. Not close enough, not fast enough...just not enough. "More. I want more."

"I'll give it to you, I swear." He touched her, a soothing stroke, while determination filled his expression. "But for your first time, slowly. With care. And I need to make sure you're protected."

She wanted to argue, but couldn't. She was too swept up in the moment. He disappeared briefly. When he returned, she realized he must have brought a condom with him...just in case. He returned to the bed and his mouth came down on hers, the gentle joining of lips and tongue at odds with the fierce hunger that underscored it. There was a familiarity to their kiss, as though they instinctively understood each other's needs and wants and were intent on supplying it. It took them to a new, unexpected level of intimacy. Passionate, yet generous. Arousing, yet open and vulnerable.

He cupped her breasts, teasing them into hard peaks with tongue and teeth. All the while he whispered the most exquisite words of love, the soft Italian making them all the more beautiful. He pressed kisses slowly downward, over her quivering belly and lower still. She gripped his shoulders to stop him.

"Don't." He interlaced her fingers with his. "Let me know you. All of you."

He reared back, so dying sunlight spilled across her, exposing her. She gazed into his black eyes and her heart rate kicked up, a fierce pounding in her ears as she waited for his reaction, waited to see what he'd do next. A slow smile curved his mouth, one of love and intense pleasure. Without taking his eyes off her, he lowered his head to her abdomen again and kissed her, sliding steadily lower.

She shuddered beneath the intimate touch feathering across her belly. With each lingering kiss, liquid heat splashed across her skin, the warmth of his breath fanned flames outward in ever-growing waves.

"I can't get enough of you," he murmured. "I don't think I ever will."

His comment arrowed straight to her soul, so beautiful and so painful. If it hadn't been for The Inferno, she'd have taken such delight and joy in the words. But she'd never know whether his reaction came from the brand of their Inferno connection or whether it came from the heart of the man.

While desire built, tears filled her eyes, overflowed, leaving hot, wet tracks behind as they slid across her temples and lost their way in her hair. She wanted this man. Wanted to love him and be loved by him. She tugged at him needing the reassurance of his kiss. He gave in to her silent demand and slid upward, the friction of skin on skin whipping up a more powerful storm of raw need. Did it really matter which part of this night was Inferno and which part real? She'd take what he gave her. Rejoice in it. Give herself over to it. And give everything she had in return.

She cupped his face and took his mouth, welcoming him inward. Wrapped him up in arms and legs and endless heat. Fueled a blaze that exploded into a need beyond anything she'd ever imagined. It ran rampant through her veins, filling her very heart and soul. She slid her hands downward to the masculine source of his desire. Cupped him. Slid her fingers over and around him.

"I love you," she told him, squeezing gently. "Please, Constantine. Don't make me wait any longer."

His breath roared from his lungs. "*Cavolo!* Do you have any idea what you're doing to me?" The question escaped through clenched teeth, his Italian so low and desperate she almost didn't understand.

Her mouth tilted upward in a teasing smile. "How could I know since I've never done this before?"

"You learn fast, *piccola*." His gaze warned of retribution. "Allow me to return the favor."

Before she could draw breath enough to respond, he cupped the warm center of her, slipping inward as he had at the lake and teasing her with slow, deliberate strokes. She bowed upward with a soft cry, desperate for his possession but not quite sure how to force the taking. She felt again the telltale flutter, the helpless clenching that would shoot her over the edge. He opened her then, slipping between her legs.

"This was always meant to be," he told her. "Call it fate. Call it The Inferno. You and I were always destined to come together. This couldn't end any other way."

He took her then with a single stroke. Gentle. Powerful. Unyielding. He sheathed himself in the warmth of her body. He moved with her in a primal rhythm as old as mankind. But it wasn't a simple sexual act. It was so much more than that. She could feel the connection in her heart, in her blood and bones, in her very soul. Where once they'd been separate and apart, empty and alone, now they were joined by an unbreakable bond.

Gianna gave herself over to the moment, reveling in it, wishing it would never end. But the rising tide couldn't be turned back. It rose faster and faster, sweeping her along, tumbling her over and over. She felt the odd flutter from before, the flutter becoming a ripple, then a hard, fisting pressure. Unable to help herself, she shattered, safe within Constantine's arms.

He surged home, his hands buried in her hair, his eyes blazing with the strength of his passion and desire. His climax hit, hard on the heels of her own. And as the final rays of the day slipped from the room, he greeted the onslaught of night with a bellow of pure, raw pleasure.

In that timeless transition between night and day, they became one. Forever changed. Forever bonded. Forever mated.

Constantine had no idea how many hours passed before he woke. The darkness was dense and rich, suggesting the blackest, most silent hour of the night. He left the warm nest the two of them had created in the bed and retreated to his room. It only took a moment to feel his way to his overnight bag and find what he needed. Then he returned to Gianna. Returned to where he belonged.

She still slept. He could just make out her sleeping form, the paleness of her skin reflecting the softest of glows from the sickle moon peeking in through the window. Her mass of hair tumbled over the pillow and down her back. And her arm was stretched out across the mattress as though reaching for him, even in deepest sleep.

Gently he took her hand in his and slipped his ring on her finger. Despite the dark, it glittered, tossing off shards of brilliant fire. Then it seemed to quiet, as though content that their final bond was near completion. Satisfied, he returned to the bed and to her arms. And to sleep.

He woke again just before dawn, something alerting him to the emptiness beside him. He was out of the bed in a flash. He didn't need to check the cabin to know she'd gone. A glance outside revealed his Porsche sitting right where he'd left it. That left the woods or the lake. The instant he thought of the lake, understanding hit.

So did fear.

He took off at a dead run, shooting through the cabin, out onto the porch. He didn't waste time with the steps, but vaulted over the railing and raced flat-out for the beach. The splinter of moon was setting, flinging the last of its fitful light at the lake, silvering the mirror-flat surface. A shape broke the liquid smoothness, moving steadily out toward the raft anchored offshore.

He dove into the water and stroked toward her, torpedoing through the water on an intercept course. He caught her just as she reached the raft. She heaved herself upward, every bit as naked as he was, and flopped onto the painted wooden boards, breathing hard. He followed her up, keeping a careful distance so he didn't give in to impulse and strangle her.

When he'd recovered his temper and had himself under complete control, he demanded, "Have you lost your damned mind?"

"Did you know you always speak in Italian whenever you're angry?"

"I'm not angry," he roared. Okay, maybe he didn't have his temper under complete control, but given the circumstances… "What the hell were you thinking, Gianna?"

She sat up. Her breathing hadn't quite returned to normal and her breasts rose and fell, a temptation beyond measure. "I was thinking that I needed to see if I really had gotten over my fear."

"Why didn't you wake me? Why sneak out on your own?"

"If I'd asked you to come with me I wouldn't have known if I wasn't afraid because you were with me, or if I'd really overcome my fear of the water." She spoke gently, as though to a cranky child, which only made him all the more cranky.

"And if you hadn't overcome your fear?" For some reason he was still roaring. "You could have drowned."

"Mmm." She had the nerve to wrinkle her nose at him and smile. "But I would have died happy."

"You think this is a *joke?*"

Her smile faded. "Of course not. I'm sorry I frightened you." She held out her hand. "Look what I found on my finger when I woke."

It was clearly an attempt to change the subject. He fought for patience. "*Piccola,* do you not see that your impulsiveness will one day get you into serious trouble? David. This swim. Please, I beg of you. For the sake of my sanity, would you try to think before acting?"

She shrugged, her breasts bobbing with the movement. "I'll try. Not sure how successful I'll be." Catching the direction of his gaze, she leaned in. "Just so you know, I'm thinking of being impulsive again."

"Dio," he muttered faintly.

"Consider yourself formally notified that I'm about to jump off the raft and swim for shore, where I will impulsively make love to the first man who catches me." She lifted an eyebrow. "Or would you rather I resist the impulse?"

He snatched her into his arms. "Feel free to resist. I, on the other hand, will not."

Together, they tumbled into the water. It took them a long, long time to reach shore. By the time they did, Gianna was no longer the least bit afraid of the water.

Nine

Gianna and Constantine returned to the city in time to join the Dante family for their weekly Sunday-night dinner at Primo's. She was pleased to discover Juice there when they showed off her ring, since it meant she could rub his winning the engagement pool in Rafe's face.

The reaction to their news was loudly celebrated for a solid hour while she and Constantine were inundated by every last family member, all toasting and laughing, offering hugs as freely as marital advice.

When it was Juice's turn, he studied her in concern. "Man, G, I hope you didn't take me seriously when I said you'd have a better shot at my finding Brimstone if you got engaged this weekend."

She glared at him in outrage. *"What?"* she demanded in an infuriated undertone. "You mean I didn't have to agree to marry this guy, after all? You would have found Brimstone for me, anyway? Juice, how *could* you?"

He stared at her, his dark eyes wide with shock. "Aw, hell. Okay, okay. Give me a sec here." He scrubbed his massive hands over his face. "Look. Let me talk to Primo. I'll explain everything, I swear. Maybe he'll just maim me a bit instead of killing me outright."

She let him suffer for a second longer, then grinned. "Man, you are *so* easy. I'm kidding, Juice." She patted his trembling arm and leaned in. "Consider that payback for our last meeting."

His bald head bobbed up and down. "Okay. Payback. I can handle payback." He shot her a look of abashed admiration. "Boy, you Dantes play rough."

Gianna gave a decisive nod. "Don't you forget it."

The next several weeks flew by. She and Constantine both decided on the earliest possible wedding date. Why wait? They'd been apart for so long and wanted each other so desperately that a lengthy engagement seemed not just pointless, but cruel.

After the big announcement, Gianna was instantly swept up in a whirlwind round of shopping and wedding preparation, while Constantine worked day and night at Romano Restoration to clear his calendar for the honeymoon. Between handling proposals for new projects and making the ongoing revisions to the Diamondt account, not to mention the various wedding demands on both their time, she often felt as though they never had a private moment to themselves. Fortunately the Diamondt account and Juice inadvertently came to their rescue.

"Remember when I told you that I might need to fly up to Seattle to meet with Gabe Moretti?" Constantine asked the question over an increasingly rare dinner engagement.

"Sure." She pulled an abbreviated rundown from memory. "Diamondt account. Son-in-law. Deceased wife. Owns her share of the family business."

He saluted her in admiration. "Impressive."

Gianna topped off their glasses of wine. "I don't suppose you're going anytime soon?"

"As a matter of fact, I am." He lifted an eyebrow. "Any chance you can break away from the wedding madness and come with me?"

She offered him a slow smile. "Every chance. As a matter of fact, I was about to ask you a similar question. I just got a lead on Brimstone. Juice contacted me about it today. He's traced the Nancy doll to Seattle."

He eyed her over the rim of his glass. "Don't tell me you're planning to go up there and mug some poor, unsuspecting little girl?"

She chuckled. "That's the general idea. Assuming David hasn't gotten there ahead of me."

She didn't dare tell him the other part of her arrangement with Juice and her brothers. If Constantine found out about that, he'd put a fast stop to a brilliant idea and she flat-out wouldn't allow him to circumvent her plans. Besides, unlike her early morning swim in the lake, she wasn't acting impulsively. She and Juice and her brothers were acting very, very carefully.

Darkness settled over Constantine's expression at the mention of David's name. "I gather you heard d'Angelo's back in town."

She nodded. "Keeping a very low profile from what I understand."

"That might have something to do with the fact that rumors are running rampant around town about some monetary discrepancies."

Gianna smiled without humor. "I guess that means no suite at the Ritz." With luck, the next suite he occupied would be at the nearest penitentiary.

"What is your family planning to do about him?"

"I know what they'd like to do." She also knew what they were *going* to do.

Constantine's gaze turned bitter cold. "They're not the only ones."

"For now, we wait." She stressed the *we*. "Juice is working the problem. Knowing him, he'll find something that'll hang David out to dry."

She could tell Constantine wanted to act, find a way to bring David down himself. Fortunately Juice and Luc were already on top of that aspect of the plan. With luck, it would all be resolved to everyone's satisfaction before much longer. That way she wouldn't have to worry about Constantine taking matters into his own hands. The idea of his getting hold of David sent shivers down her spine. She couldn't risk that happening. Not with Constantine's temper.

He continued to chew on the information. "I heard the International Banking Association has rescinded the award they were going to give the d'Angelos."

"Couldn't happen to a nicer family." She leaned across the table and caught Constantine's hand in her own. Her engagement ring flashed with the same heat and fire that characterized The Inferno. "Forget about David. Let's talk about our trip to Seattle. How long will you be hung up in meetings?"

His gaze sparked. "I'll make sure we have plenty of private time. And speaking of private time…" He shoved aside his half-finished dinner. "I can think of far more important activities than eating. Food can wait. This can't."

A teasing smile played across her mouth. "And what would 'this' be?"

"I see you need a short refresher course." He lifted her out of her chair and carried her in the direction of his bedroom.

"No." Her arms tightened around his neck. "I need a very, very, *very* long one."

Gianna and Constantine flew to Seattle Friday night after work and checked into the Crown, a brand-new hotel within walking distance of the piers, Pike Place Market and the main shopping center. He'd somehow snagged a suite with a stunning western view of the sound and mountains.

After a late dinner, they retreated to the bedroom and silently stripped away their clothes. The room was dark and cool, lit only by the lights of the city and a full moon filtering through a bank of clouds hanging just over the Olympic Mountains. It shimmered across Elliott Bay and slid into the room, gilding the bed in silver.

Unable to resist, she approached and flung herself into his arms for a kiss that expressed all the pent-up desire and frustration that seemed to define their relationship up until now. Her body impacted against the hard, taut lines of his. This kiss proved no different than any of the others. She didn't just surrender, but gave herself up to him. Utterly. It had always been like that between them. She didn't think it could be any other way.

"It's only you. You're the only one it's ever been," she told him.

"Or ever could be?"

The question dropped between them and she closed her eyes against the hard knowledge glimmering within his dark gaze. "I'm sorry. I wish I could answer that question for you," she whispered.

"It doesn't matter." But he'd replied in Italian, giving himself away. "Nor does it change the fact that we're connected, you and I. We have been since the moment we first touched."

It was true, she acknowledged. She came alive whenever

he took her into his arms. When he kissed her. She could practically feel her nerve endings fire, throbbing with excitement, urging her to do things that should have shocked her to the core…and didn't.

He groaned. "Why? Why you and no one else?"

Gianna shook her head, struggling to clear it of the sensual fog with only limited success. She understood his question. It was one she'd asked herself often enough. "I have no idea why," she admitted.

She simply knew that being in Constantine's arms felt right. More, it felt necessary. Necessary to her very existence, whether she wanted it that way or not. Constantine slid his hands into her hair and lifted her closer, deepening the kiss. He was like a man who'd fasted for months, even though it had only been days since they'd last spent the night together. He gazed down at her as though he'd been presented with a delectable banquet, one he couldn't resist. A whispered moan of surrender slipped from her and he breathed it in.

Together they fell back on the bed and she gave herself over to his touch. He stroked her breasts, gently plucking at her painfully sensitive nipples. His calloused fingertips tripped downward, sweeping along her abdomen, then his mouth followed the path his hands took. When he reached the core of her, he scooped his large hands beneath her bottom and lifted her. Took her. Drove her straight over the top. She arched upward and exploded helplessly. Endlessly.

And then he mated his body to hers and took her again.

It was beyond anything she'd experienced before. He called to her in a language that blended English with Italian, sweet words, a tumble of demands, hoarse pleas. She clung to him, moved with him. Drove him as he'd just driven her. Sent him soaring. Up, up, up. And there they teetered before slamming together over the next pinnacle and plummeting into oblivion.

Spent, they curled together, drawing comfort and sustenance, one from the other. And they slept; a sleep of sweet hopes and dreams, wrapped together so tightly two melded into one.

Gianna woke again in the dead of night. The full moon was sinking behind the Olympic Mountains, setting the peaks aglow and silvering the room with its light. At some point Constantine had spooned her against the hard curve of his body. While the moon softened the appearance of the room, it sculpted Constantine's muscles and sinew into granite.

She could tell the instant he woke. The tenor of his breathing changed, deepened, and his hold on her tightened ever so slightly. "What time do you need to get up tomorrow?" she asked.

"Early."

"When are you meeting Moretti?"

He chuckled. "Not so early." He swept her hair to one side and traced a kiss along the back of her neck. "I want time to go through the building and finalize my presentation before we get together. Why don't you join me there around four?"

She shivered beneath his gently insistent touch. "At Diamondt's?"

"Sure." He caught the lobe of her ear between his teeth and tugged, giving a husky laugh at her helpless shudder. "I can introduce you to Moretti. Since this is the first time he and I are meeting face-to-face, maybe it'll help put us on a more friendly footing."

"Okay."

"What about you?" Constantine asked.

"I want to check out the address Juice gave me." She forced her muscles to remain relaxed, difficult enough when he kept touching her. Even so, she couldn't risk communicating any of her tension to him.

"I wish you'd wait until I can go with you," he murmured against her ear.

Oh, Lord. That would be a disaster. "No time," she hastened to say. "We're flying home right after your meeting, aren't we?"

He considered for a minute, his hand stroking her in an absentminded way. Unfortunately there was nothing absentminded about her reaction to his touch. She turned in his arms to face him and slid her leg over top of his. "Okay, fine," he said at last. "But call me right before and right after you speak to this woman."

She nipped at his mouth. "No problem."

She didn't give him the chance to say anything else. The sooner they put the conversation to rest, the better. Of course, the instant he shifted her beneath him, she found she couldn't think, much less speak.

They gave themselves over to one another, gave themselves over to the night. Her soft sigh of pleasure was answered by his hoarse demand. Her cry of completion echoed his roar of satisfaction. Through the night they burned, riding the crest of passion from one wave to the next until the first break of dawn tumbled them back into a deep sleep.

The next morning Gianna woke to discover Constantine long gone. He'd left a single red rose on the pillow beside her and she picked it up, smiling softly. Even better, he'd prepared a pot of coffee for her, using one of Seattle's world-renowned brands. She sipped in appreciation while preparing for the day. After doing a swift run-through with first Luc and then Juice, she pulled out the bold red slacks and jacket she'd chosen specifically for today's mission.

Next, she headed downstairs, speaking at length to the concierge and getting very specific directions to the address she'd been given. She arranged for a cab, requesting it pick her up in half an hour. Then she returned to her room and sat, counting down the minutes, before returning to the lobby. The hope was that the brief delay would give David time to bribe the concierge and obtain the address, or if that failed, follow her to her destination. Once Luc and Juice spotted him, they'd arrange their men in a tidy net around the house, ready to spring the trap when David made his move.

Since it was midday Saturday, the drive to White Center didn't take long. The taxi cruised slowly through a neighborhood overrun with small boxy homes. Though there was an air of shabbiness that encompassed many, for the most part they were tidy with neatly kept lawns and flower beds.

At the last minute she remembered to call Constantine. "I found the house. At least, I think I have."

"Give me the address."

She hesitated. "Why do you need the address?"

"So I know where to send the police if I don't hear from you within the next thirty minutes."

She sighed and did as he requested. "There's no need to worry, Constantine," she reassured. "This will be over before you know it and I'll call you the minute it is."

"What do you mean?" Constantine asked sharply.

"Oh, well, you know," she said, a trifle distracted. "It won't take long to discuss the situation with Mrs. Mereaux. I'm sure Primo will pay her a generous price for Brimstone and that'll be that."

"Gianna—"

"Oh, someone's looking out the window. I have to go. I'll call you as soon as I'm done."

She flipped the cell phone closed before he could say anything further and exited the cab.

Constantine stared down at his cell phone and frowned. Something about his conversation with Gianna felt off, and a sense of wrongness sizzled through him. He glanced at the group hovering over the blueprints spread across a table in the center of the Diamondt building foyer. Getting the account was vital to Romano Restoration's continued growth and expansion. Maybe that explained why he'd been so distracted. So distracted that he hadn't really given his full attention to this Brimstone business.

But now that he did...

It hit him then and he swore, praying he was wrong. He flipped open his phone and dialed Luc's number. No answer.

Juice's number. No answer.

Rafe. Draco. No answer.

He barked an excuse to the men waiting for him and took off at a dead run. Why was it that his future wife always had him running? Even worse, why was it always in terror that something horrible had happened to her?

Gianna knocked on the front door of the Mereaux residence. It opened a moment later and a woman of mixed race, slightly younger than herself, greeted her. She eyed Gianna nervously.

"How long are we supposed to stand here?" she asked, a strong hint of Louisiana Cajun clear in her voice. "I'm sort of new at all this."

Gianna smiled. "Me, too. I think we just need to talk for a minute or two. I'm Gianna, by the way."

"Mia." They shook hands.

"I'm surprised Juice allowed you to do this, Mia. He tends to be very protective about innocents, as he calls us. He was forced to enlist my help or David wouldn't have taken the bait. But you…"

Mia grimaced. "No choice. They had some other woman all set to pretend to be me, but Mr. d'Angelo got the jump on 'em. Nearly caught Mr. Juice standing right over yonder in my front parlor."

"David was here already?" Gianna asked, shocked.

"Surely was." Mia stepped back as planned and allowed Gianna to enter. "Fortunately Mr. Juice had time to hide in the kitchen. And my neighbor was here to take my daughter, Bebelle, for the day. She had her children with her—all five. That d'Angelo man couldn't do much with all them witnesses, now could he? So, he made up some fine excuse about a wrong address and left. Since he'd seen me, I insisted on staying put until they could arrest him."

Gianna closed the door behind her. "I'm so sorry, Mia. We all thought David would follow me. He must have gotten the address from the concierge, instead, and come straight over. So much for careful planning."

"That's what Mr. Juice said." A hint of warmth touched her cheekbones. "He wanted to pull the plug, but I wouldn't let him. Can't risk that man coming back thinking the doll is still here, now can I? That wouldn't be safe for my Bebelle."

"Well, this won't take long. We'll just let David take the doll and our part will be over." Gianna threw an arm around Mia's shoulders and gave her a swift hug. "Are you nervous?"

"A little," Mia admitted. "My main concern is Bebelle. Mr. Juice has assured me any number of times that she's safe with my neighbor."

Gianna grinned, sensing Mia felt more than a passing interest in Mr. Juice. "Well, if Juice said it, you can believe it."

"Would you like something to drink?"

"No, thanks." She wandered over to the couch where the Nancy doll perched and glanced over her shoulder at Mia. "May I?"

"Oh, sure. Help yourself."

"How did you end up with her, anyway?"

Mia shrugged. "It was shortly after my husband died. Bebelle just cried and cried she missed her daddy so bad. One day this strange child came up to her and just put that Nancy doll right in my little girl's arms. Said Bebelle needed it more than she did. Said it was a magical doll and would bring her happiness. And once it did, she should give it away to someone else in need." Mia turned her great, dark eyes on Gianna. "You think she's right? You think it'll bring my Bebelle happiness?"

"Yes, as a matter of fact, I think it will."

Gianna picked up the doll just as a heavy knock sounded on the front door. She stiffened, knowing full well who they'd find there.

Constantine tried Gianna's cell phone for the umpteenth time since flagging down the taxi. The cabbie drove as fast as he dared, the sizable tip thrown his way aiding in breaking a few speeding laws. That didn't change the fact that when he got his hands on his future wife—not to mention his future brothers-in-law—there would be hell to pay. He tried Luc's number again. Juice. Nothing from any of them.

He allowed fury to triumph over panic. It was the only way he could keep from going insane. Hadn't they discussed her impulsiveness at the lake? Hadn't he explained in no uncertain terms that it wasn't a quality he appreciated? Now he understood where it came from. It must be a genetic anomaly that ran down the entire Dante line. Though how that explained Juice, he couldn't say. Maybe it rubbed off with prolonged association.

"This is the street," the cabdriver said, pointing. "But the cops have it blocked. Are we too late, do you think?"

Constantine must have replied in Italian because the driver frowned in confusion. He fought to find the appropriate words in English, couldn't come up with them. Instead he peeled off a number of notes and tossed them in the driver's direction. He was out of the car in a flash.

Please, God, no. Not Gianna. He couldn't survive without Gianna. She was his mate. His heart. His life. He loved her more than he thought it possible to love anyone. If something had happened to her... He picked up his speed.

The police stopped him a few houses before the address Gianna had given him. It took endless minutes to make himself understood, to find the appropriate words in the appropriate language to convince them that he belonged on the other side of their blockade. That his future wife was involved. That she needed him, and only him.

Someone down the line waved him through and he took off at a swift jog. Luc stood talking to a police officer. Gianna was nowhere to be seen. He charged toward her brother and would have taken him down if his bride-to-be hadn't chosen that moment to come flying out of the house and straight into his arms.

"Constantine!" She wrapped her arms tight around his neck. "You'll never believe what happened."

"I'll tell you what's going to happen," he growled, snatching her close and enclosing her in a hold she wouldn't soon escape. "I'm going to knock your brother on his ass."

"I'd really rather you wouldn't. Listen to me." She caught

his face between her hands and forced him to look at her. "I said listen to me, Constantine. They caught David. He's in police custody. I don't think he's going to get out of this one, thanks to Brimstone."

Luc approached, a huge grin on his face. "You should have been here, Romano." He slapped Constantine on his back. "You could have helped us take d'Angelo down."

"Let go of me, Gianna," Constantine demanded.

She clung tighter. "Not if you plan on hitting my brother."

"I said, let go of me."

Luc's attention switched from one to the other, a frown forming between his brows. "I don't understand. What's the problem?"

"What's the…" It took Constantine a moment to recover his breath enough to speak. He seized Gianna around the waist and set her to one side. "How would you like my putting Téa in the sort of danger you've put Gianna in? What would you do to the man who used her in such a fashion and never discussed it with you first?"

Luc froze. For a split second, his gaze landed on Gianna then bounced off again. "You're absolutely right, Constantine. I apologize. I was so anxious to get my hands on d'Angelo that I didn't even think about the risk my sister was taking. I guess I'm so used to the security business it never occurred to me that she'd be in any danger."

Constantine closed his eyes, his fury deflating. "You thought I knew," he said to Luc.

Gianna's brother winced and shot him a look of intense sympathy. "Yeah, sorry. Should have known better. Gia has seven older brothers and cousins, all of whom set a horrible example for her. There's not a trick she hasn't learned."

"I'll keep that in mind from now on."

"Still, I should have spoken directly to you about it."

"Are you very angry?" Gianna had the nerve to ask.

"Furious." Constantine spared her a brief, speaking glance. "We'll discuss it later. Right now I have some very confused businessmen waiting for me."

"I've already given my statement to the police." She checked with Luc, who nodded. "I can leave now, if you'd like."

If he'd like? Words fought for release, none of them fit to be aired. "I don't like," he said gently. "I insist."

She cleared her throat, perhaps becoming aware of the extent of his anger for the first time. "Great." She plastered a cheerful smile on her face and glanced around. "So, how do we get there?"

It was only then that Constantine realized he'd paid off the cab. Luc jumped in and waved Juice over, who waited on the tiny front stoop of the Mereaux house, hovering protectively over the slender woman standing beside him. "You can use our rental while we go to the police station and finalize everything."

Luc had chosen a nondescript sedan and Constantine helped Gianna into the car. He managed to drive a full dozen blocks before he couldn't stand it any longer and pulled over. His hands clenched around the steering wheel. "Okay, let's hear it."

Gianna sighed. "I'm sorry, Constantine. I knew if I told you what we planned, you wouldn't agree."

"Wouldn't agree?" he repeated. He swiveled in his seat to face her. "Have you lost your mind? *Of course* I wouldn't have agreed. I'd never do anything to put you in jeopardy or allowed you anywhere near d'Angelo, especially after what he did to you last time."

A stubborn look settled on her face. "Don't you see? I had to face him the same way I had to face the lake. Luc and Juice wouldn't have let anything happen to me. And the police were alerted in advance. They had officers in the area." She caught her lower lip between her teeth, her jade gaze holding a combination of apology and determination. "I did it, Constantine. I looked him right in the eyes and realized what a contemptible little worm he is."

Constantine fought to temper his anger, to consider the situation from her point of view. "I can't argue with your description. I can and do argue with how you went about it. Did you give a single thought to my take on all this? To how I'd react or my opinion? We're supposed to be a team, Gianna."

She winced. "You're right and I am sorry. I promise I won't keep anything from you in the future. Not that anything like this will ever happen again."

"No, it won't, as I intend to make very clear to each and every one of your relatives." He couldn't help himself. He pulled her close and held her. "Were you very afraid?"

"Not even a little." She tilted her head back and grinned. "Okay, maybe a little, but it was only a very little."

"D'Angelo followed you to the Mereaux residence?"

"More or less. He arrived a few minutes after I did."

"He didn't harm you or the Mereaux woman?"

"No. Mia handled it like a trouper. He came in and demanded the doll. Luc had told us what to say so it would be a clear-cut case of theft." Her brow wrinkled. "Or is it burglary?" She shrugged. "No matter. They taped every last word. Then David ripped open the poor doll and removed Brimstone. Lord, it was huge. And because it's worth so much, taking it makes it a far more serious crime. Somehow I don't think he's going to get out of this one as easily as he's gotten out of so many of his other problems."

"He won't be getting out of those, either. He and his father are under investigation for embezzlement."

"Couldn't happen to a nicer guy," Gianna said cheerfully.

Constantine checked his watch. "Moretti should be arriving shortly. I need to get back to the Diamondt building."

"I gather I'm coming with you?" she asked.

He shot her a hard look. "You, *piccola,* will not be out of my sight for the rest of our stay in Seattle."

She sighed. "Sort of thought you might say that."

Gianna and Constantine arrived at the Diamondt building shortly after four. To her intense surprise, the first person she saw when she entered the foyer was her oldest cousin, Sev. She made a beeline for him.

"Severo Dante, what on earth are you doing here?" she demanded.

He jerked at her question and swept around to confront her. She checked her forward momentum at the last instant, only just preventing herself from giving the man a hug.

He was as tall as Sev—two or three inches over six feet—with hair every bit as black. He also possessed the same intense golden eyes as both her cousin and her grandfather, Primo. His features were equally hard, cut in strong, less-than-handsome lines, but all the more powerful because of it. He'd dressed in a black suit, one that emphasized his broad shoulders and strong, muscular legs, and cloaked him in darkness.

Unable to help herself, she fell back a step, thoroughly intimidated. "I'm sorry. I thought you were my cousin." She glanced over her shoulder, searching for Constantine, before offering her hand with a hesitant smile. "I don't suppose you have any Dante relatives in your background? You could pass for one of my family without any problem at all. The resemblance is really quite amazing."

He didn't speak for a long moment. Then in a voice as-deep and black as his appearance, he asked, "Who are you?"

Her hand dropped slowly to her side. "I'm Gianna Dante. Constantine Romano is my fiancé," she explained stiffly.

His eyes narrowed in open displeasure. To her extreme relief, she felt the reassuring pressure of Constantine's hands on her shoulder. "Is there a problem?"

Moretti hesitated, then shook his head. "I'm satisfied with what I've seen here. Send the contract," he said, his gaze never shifting from Gianna. And with that, he turned and left, flowing from the building like black fog.

"What the hell was that about?" Constantine demanded.

"I think I remember where I heard the name Moretti before," Gianna murmured, stricken. "That's the name of the woman my uncle Dominic had an affair with. The woman he was leaving Aunt Laura for. Oh, Constantine. I think maybe Uncle Dominic did more than have an affair with her. A lot more."

Ten

Constantine stared after Gabe Moretti in disbelief. "You think he's a Dante? Seriously?"

"I don't know." Gianna gnawed on her lower lip. "You saw him. Don't you think he could have passed for Sev's twin brother?"

"Don't jump to any rash conclusions," Constantine warned. "You're far too good at that."

She swiveled to face him, planting her hands on her shapely hips. "Tell me you're not going to rub that in my face for the rest of our lives."

The time had come to deal with her impulsiveness once and for all. He approached and went toe-to-toe with her. "I won't rub it in your face, if you promise not to act rashly."

She smiled sweetly. "I assume that means you want prior approval on every decision I make. How deliciously caveman of you." She swept her hand downward to indicate her pantsuit. "Would you care to approve my clothes, for instance? My shoes? What about my hair?"

"That's not what I mean and you damn well know it," he growled. "Even Luc acknowledged that I should have been informed of what you had planned for today. You admitted that the only reason you didn't was that you knew I would object. So don't act as though I'm coming on like some sort of Neanderthal." He leaned in. "Imagine if the situation had been reversed and I'd been the one in that house. If Juice and your brothers had kept our plan from you. Admit it. You would have been furious."

For an instant, he thought she'd argue the point. Then she blew out a sigh and nodded. "No, you're right. I should have told you, just as I would have expected you to tell me."

A smile built across his face. It was times like this that she blew him away. Her fairness. The frank way she admitted her mistakes. They were just a few of the qualities he adored about her. "I appreciate your honesty."

"Yeah, well. I'm still sort of new at this whole team thing we have going," she admitted.

"As am I." He cupped a hand around the back of her neck and drew her up for a slow kiss. "Look on the bright side. D'Angelo is in jail and unlikely to get out anytime soon. I was just awarded a huge contract. And you may have a new cousin."

She grimaced. "I'm not sure there's a bright side to your last point."

"Time will tell." He released her. "Now that we're a team, how do you suggest we handle the possibility?"

"I don't know," she admitted.

"Should you tell Primo?"

"Tell him that his son may have fathered a child out of wedlock?" She shuddered. "Scary thought."

"Do you want to think about it for a while?"

Her eyebrows shot skyward. "What? Not act impulsively for once? Me?"

He smothered a smile. "I know it'll be a challenge."

"In this case, not so much." She frowned unhappily. "To be honest, I would like to think about it for a while."

Constantine glanced again at the exit Gabe Moretti had taken. "I have a feeling you won't be the only one."

The next several weeks passed with lightning speed. Gianna should have been blissfully happy, but a single shadow continued to hang over her. Not once in all the time she'd been with Constantine had he said those vital three words she'd shared with him the night they'd made love for the first time: *I love you.* He wanted her. No question there. The Inferno burned and connected them in ways that suggested love and a lifelong commitment. But real love? Natural love? Non-Inferno influenced love?

She just couldn't be certain.

How much of his desire and commitment to marry her were based on The Inferno and feeling honor-bound to marry her because they'd made love? And how much of it was based on true feeling? It was definitely a conversation they needed to have before the wedding.

But as the days and weeks passed, Gianna couldn't figure out a way to discuss the problem with him. Or perhaps she couldn't find the right words because, despite facing all of her other fears, she couldn't bring herself to face this one. She couldn't bear the idea of his admitting to her that he didn't love her, that it was all due to The Inferno.

If that's what he believed, she'd be forced to cancel their wedding, something her entire family—not to mention Constantine—would oppose. Oppose? She laughed without humor. She knew her family. And though they were the most loving and generous people she'd ever known, they wouldn't hesitate to drag her to the altar and find a priest who'd marry them regardless of whether or not she said "I do." Considering she and Constantine had experienced The Inferno, they wouldn't give her any other choice. If they knew the two of them had slept together... Well, forget it. The wedding would happen faster than the sizzle of The Inferno.

And still the days passed.

The night before the wedding, Primo threw a party in their honor. "I think it was to keep us from stealing away your fiancé and debauching him," Rafe informed Gianna with a wink.

She laughed. "No bachelor's party?"

"We might try to sneak him off into a corner and debauch him there. Maybe Primo won't notice."

"Doubtful. Primo notices everything and knows everything."

Though there was one thing he didn't know. She hadn't told him about Gabe Moretti, yet. Both she and Constantine had made some subtle inquiries after their return from Seattle. At least, she hoped they'd been subtle. Eventually, they'd discovered that Gabe Moretti was indeed the son of Cara Moretti. And though that fact alone didn't prove Dominic Dante was his father, the family resemblance suggested that possibility. Possibility? Probability. After discussing it with Constantine a final time, she'd decided to turn the entire matter over to her grandfather.

She found him where she often did, in the kitchen. He'd chased off all his helpers and she knew better than to offer her assistance. In this family, the kitchen was her grandfather's domain. "So, *chiacchierona*. Are you nervous about tomorrow?" he asked, his trademark cigar clamped between his teeth.

She hesitated, driven to answer honestly. "A little."

Her grandfather sampled his sauce, eyeing her over the steaming ladle. "And what part makes you a little nervous?"

"Constantine and I haven't known each other very long."

Primo lifted a shoulder in a shrug. "Eh. You have the next sixty years to get to know each other. You have The Inferno, which means your marriage will be passionate, happy and successful. That is all that matters, yes?"

She stared down at the kitchen table and traced one of the gouges her cousin Marco had carved in it years ago. A love scratch, her grandmother had claimed. A nick alongside so many other nicks, all of which helped imbue a piece of furniture with the richness and history of the family who owned it. Gianna smiled sadly. Maybe she wouldn't be as nervous of tomorrow's events if she believed that The Inferno was forever, that someday she and Constantine would have a kitchen table that spoke of generations worth of love and use.

She glanced up, on the verge of telling her grandfather about what she'd learned on her thirteenth birthday. But when she looked into those ancient golden eyes, eyes filled with love and understanding and an absolute certainty in the world as he knew it, she couldn't bring herself to disillusion him.

"Constantine and I met someone in Seattle," she said instead. "I didn't know if I should tell you about it. But I think I better."

Primo turned the flame beneath his sauce to a simmer and snagged a pair of bottles of homemade beer out of the cavernous refrigerator. Popping the tops with practiced ease, he set one in front of her. He took the seat beside her and tapped his bottle against hers. *"Cin cin."*

They both drank. "This man…" She didn't see any easy way to tell him. "He looked just like Sev. And you."

Primo closed his eyes. "His name?"

"Gabe Moretti. He wasn't pleased to meet me." She waited for her grandfather to gather himself before continuing. "Who is he? How is he related to us?"

"I believe he is your Uncle Dominic's son."

It confirmed her suspicions. "With the woman he was leaving Aunt Laura for?"

"This is not an appropriate conversation on the eve of your wedding," Primo said gently. "We will talk of it another time. Thank you for telling me."

She recognized Primo's expression. She wouldn't get any more information out of him. "I'm planning on holding you to that. If Constantine's going to do business with the man, chances are we'll meet again—sooner rather than later. I'd rather not be in the dark when we do."

Primo inclined his head. "You will not mention this to anyone else. *Mi hai capito,* Gianna Marie?"

She made a face. "Yes, I understand. In fact, I had a feeling you were going to say that." She stood. "I'll let Constantine know."

The rest of the night was everything she could have asked, the evening filled with joy, fun, laughter and, most important of all, the warmth of family unity. She wasn't the least surprised when the Dantes gathered in Primo's garden after dinner and began relating old, favorite stories. While her grandparents took turns telling Constantine about their first Inferno meeting—perpetuating the falsehood of The Inferno—Gianna slipped away from the light and crowd and retreated into the shadows.

Tomorrow she'd be a married woman. Would she be one of the lucky ones, like her own parents and grandparents? Or would she and Constantine end up like Uncle Dominic and Aunt Laura?

"Are you okay?" Constantine came up behind her and wrapped his arms around her, pulling her close.

She melted against him with a sigh of happiness. "I'm fine."

"Nervous about tomorrow?"

"You're the tenth person tonight who's asked me that."

"Probably why you're nervous."

She laughed. "That must be it." She turned in his arms and allowed her fingers to drift deep into the thick waves of his hair. "There can't possibly be any other reason."

"No, there can't." His absolute certainty humbled her. "You know I want you more than any other woman I've known."

Not quite a declaration of love. But close. Maybe in time he'd say the words. Maybe in time he'd mean them. Before she could reply, she heard Rafe just behind them, laughing at something Luc said.

He approached, slapping Constantine on the back. "Ready for tomorrow or do you have cold feet? My car's out front. They'd never catch us if you want to make a break for it."

Constantine's brow furrowed briefly as he mulled over "make a break for it." He must have reasoned through the idiom because he laughed. "No breaking necessary. Gianna is the only woman I want. The only woman I'll ever want."

Rafe chuckled. "She'll definitely be the only one. The Inferno will see to that."

Constantine's bleak gaze shifted to Gianna, making her want to weep. "So I understand," he murmured. "Let us hope the reverse is also true."

* * *

The day of Gianna's wedding dawned sunny and temperate. The morning passed in a dreamy haze. Someone came and fixed her hair, then magically vanished. Same with her makeup. While her bridesmaids—a few college friends, along with her sisters and cousins-in-law—hovered and fluttered, laughing and teasing, Nonna and her mother kept her from floating away. Or maybe it was Rafe's words that kept her grounded, slipping into her dream day like a dark, threatening cloud.

She'll definitely be the only one. The Inferno will see to that.

The gown she'd chosen was molded antique lace with a keyhole back and chapel train. The finishing touch was a fabulous Dante fire diamond tiara that kept her lace veil anchored firmly in place. The trip to the wedding chapel took no time at all, or so it seemed to Gianna. One minute she stood in her parents' home, the next she entered the church. The women were all ushered into the bride's room to await the start of the ceremony. She'd been told that Constantine and his groomsmen had already arrived and were relaxing in a nearby room. She could vaguely hear the sound of masculine voices drifting down the hall.

"Are you okay?" Ariana asked in concern. She and Lazz had flown in for the special occasion with their baby, Amata.

Gianna managed a quick smile. "Of course. No worries." Well, except for one.

She'll definitely be the only one. The Inferno will see to that.

It wasn't fair, she realized. As much as she loved Constantine, it wasn't fair to keep him trapped against his will. To force him into a marriage. Not if he didn't really love her. She didn't want an Inferno love. Not one forced on the man she married. She wanted him to love her for herself. Because he had chosen. Because he had made the decision she was the only one for him.

She shot to her feet in a panic. "I need to see Constantine."

For a split second the women all froze, silence gripping the room. Then everyone started talking at once. She couldn't make out a word they said. Nor did it matter. She headed for the door.

Her mother intercepted her, but Gianna shook her head. "Don't, Mamma. I wouldn't ask if it weren't important."

"It is bad luck," Elia protested. "You must wait until after you exchange your vows. Look, your babbo is here. The ceremony is about to begin. It's time for me to take my seat in the church."

Gianna shook her head. "This won't wait. I have to talk to Constantine now. Before the wedding."

Elia turned to her husband. "Alessandro," she called, a hint of desperation slipping into her voice. "Come speak to your daughter."

Before he could, Gianna escaped the bride's room. Her mother followed, the rest of the women on her heels. Gianna found Constantine's room without any difficulty. The door stood open. Masculine laughter erupted from inside, the sound dying the instant they caught sight of her standing in the doorway.

Constantine stood, eyeing her in concern. "*Piccola?* What are you doing here? Is something wrong?"

"I need to talk to you. It's important." She spared her brothers and cousins a swift look. She'd rather they not hear this next part. "Would you excuse us, please?"

They didn't want to leave. But they did it for her. One by one they filed from the room.

"*Dio,* look at you," Constantine murmured. "Words fail me."

Tears misted her eyes and her chin quivered. "You look pretty fine, yourself."

He must have sensed her panic because he stilled. "What's going on?" he asked sharply. "Why are you here?"

"I love you. I just need to tell you that first."

His expression relaxed and he closed the distance between them. He started to reach for her, then paused. "I'm afraid to touch you." Gently he pulled her into his arms and kissed her. "Now tell me what's wrong."

She closed her eyes. He still hadn't said the words, which made her decision so much easier. "I need to do something for you, before we marry."

"I don't understand. Do what?" He glanced briefly at the closed door. "Are you sure this can't wait?" he asked.

Almost. Almost she grabbed the lifeline. But she'd faced all of her other fears. She'd face this one, too. "No, this can't wait." She held out her hands. She could see they trembled, the fire diamond on her engagement ring flashing in agitation. "Give me your hand. Your right hand." The Infernoed hand.

His confusion threatened to break her heart, especially when she knew he didn't suspect what she was about to do. She took his strong, warm hand between her freezing ones. It took every ounce of determination she possessed to say the words that had to be spoken.

"I release you," she told him, her voice trembling. She had a vague recollection of her uncle saying it three times. Third time's the charm? Just in case, she added, "I release you. I release you."

He must have begun to suspect something. "What have you done, Gianna?" he demanded.

The breath shuddered from her lungs. "I've just released you from The Inferno."

"You've *what?*"

Tears spilled over. "I've released you."

"No." He jerked his hand free of hers. "No, you have not done this to us. *Give it back!*"

Her face crumpled. "I don't think I can."

Constantine strode to the door, flinging it open. "Get Primo. Now." He slammed the door closed and turned to confront her. "Why would you do this to us, Gianna? Why try to destroy what we have, today of all days?"

She sank onto a footstool and bowed her head. Her dress pooled around her and she ran shaking fingers over the beautiful antique lace. Such a gorgeous gown meant for such a happy occasion. And look what she'd done to it. To them.

Slowly she lifted her eyes, forcing herself to meet Constantine's infuriated gaze. "I did it because you're not the only one who believes in honor. I refuse to use The Inferno to force you to the altar. I want you to marry me because you love me, not because you have no other choice. You said yourself that you didn't like having the control taken away from you. You've even referred to The Inferno as an infection. All I've done is return your control, cured your infection."

The door burst open and Primo strode into the room. He took one look at Gianna and Constantine, and closed the door behind him. "What is this?" He spoke in Italian, the only indication of his concern. "What has happened?"

Constantine swiveled to confront him, leveling an accusing finger in Gianna's direction. "She took away The Inferno. Make her give it back."

Primo froze for an instant. Then his mouth dropped open and he blinked in astonishment. Tilting back his head, he roared with laughter. "Give it *back?*" Tears filled his eyes, making them glitter like ancient gold and he fumbled for a handkerchief to wipe the dampness from them. "Is this a joke?"

"It's no joke," Constantine said through clenched teeth. "She released me. I want you to make her give me back The Inferno."

Primo patted his pockets until he came up with a cigar. "Give it back," he repeated, still chuckling.

"Primo, you can't smoke that in here," Gianna informed him quietly. "It's against the law."

"Phft. These laws do not apply to me. I am what they call 'grandfathered in.'" But he did refrain from lighting up. He clamped the cigar between his teeth and leveled Gianna with a look. *"Spieghi lei."*

She didn't want to explain. Couldn't explain. Couldn't tell her beloved grandfather the truth about his son and daughter-in-law. Definitely couldn't tell him what she'd learned about The Inferno. "Primo—"

"Subito!"

She shrugged, surrendering to the inevitable. "Constantine's right. I took back The Inferno. I released him."

Primo raised his eyes heavenward. *"Santa Maria, Madre di Dio.* What has gotten into you, Gianna? There are no take backs in The Inferno." He wavered between laughter and outrage. "Where did you hear such nonsense?"

She hesitated. One look at her grandfather's expression warned that he'd have the answer from her, no matter how long it took. "Uncle Dominic and Aunt Laura."

Primo stiffened. "Dominic," he repeated. Spinning around, he crossed to the door and yanked it open. "Get Severo. Now."

Her cousin Sev entered a moment later. He was followed by his wife, Francesca, and Constantine's sister, Ariana.

An instant later her parents slipped into the room, along with her grandmother, Nonna. They settled her in a chair not far from Gianna. That opened the floodgates and the entire family piled in behind them.

"This concerns all of us," Alessandro informed his father. *"La famiglia."*

And that said it all.

Reluctantly Primo nodded. He took a seat beside Gianna and gathered her hands in his. Constantine sat behind her, his solid warmth at her back, a supportive hand on her shoulder. Her family encircled the three of them, love and concern flowing from them in palpable waves.

"You have often been a *chiacchierona* when you should not," Primo said, though kindly. "Perhaps this is one of the times you should have chattered more and chose instead to chatter less. From the beginning, Gianna."

She spared Sev a swift look. Other than her grandparents, his reaction to her story worried her the most. "It was my thirteenth birthday. The day before Uncle Dominic and Aunt Laura died."

Almost in unison, the family crossed themselves. "We were at your uncle's house to celebrate the occasion," Primo prompted. "I remember that day."

Her hands tightened within her grandfather's warm hold. Behind her, Constantine gave her shoulder a reassuring squeeze. "Even at that young age, I was crazy about shoes."

"So was Mamma," Sev murmured.

"Yes. For my gift, she told me to go up to her closet and pick out any pair of shoes I wanted." Gianna sighed at the memory. "I'd never seen so many lovely shoes."

Constantine snorted.

Gianna took instant umbrage. "Believe it or not, she had even more pairs than I do. And her closet…" She sighed. Aware that she was getting a bit offtrack, she forced herself to focus. "I'd probably been up there for a full hour, trying on pair after pair, unable to make up my mind, when Uncle Dominic and Aunt Laura came into the bedroom. I was buried in the closet. They didn't know I was there. Aunt Laura had probably forgotten. Or maybe she assumed I'd already left. They…they were fighting."

Sev's expression darkened. "They did that a lot right before…" He shook off the memory. "Go on, Gianna."

"Uncle Dominic told her he planned to leave and wanted a divorce. Aunt Laura started crying. She said…" Gianna swallowed. "She said 'But what about The Inferno? You told me it would last forever.'"

Sev stiffened. Primo closed his eyes. Nonna lifted a trembling hand to her mouth.

"I'm sorry," Gianna whispered. "I'm so sorry to tell you this."

"Continue," Primo prompted.

"Uncle Dominic said that he'd experienced The Inferno with someone else. If he mentioned her name, I don't recall it. He said it happens sometimes. That it was beyond his control." She felt the ripple of disbelief sweep through her cousins and brothers. She didn't dare look at any of their wives to see how they were taking the news. "Aunt Laura was still crying, but she was also angry. She said that he'd told her when they'd married that he'd felt The Inferno for her. That Primo had told her it only happened once in a lifetime. That she'd never have married him if they hadn't felt The Inferno for each other."

"The Inferno does only happen once in a lifetime," her grandfather said gently.

Gianna shook her head. She looked at him miserably, the pain of disillusioning him worse than anything she'd ever experienced before. "Uncle Dominic said you didn't know because you'd never felt it for anyone else the way he had.

He said that Dantes can feel it for more than one person, but that he could fix things. Take away The Inferno so Aunt Laura wouldn't love him anymore. He took her hand in his and he released her."

"What?" The question came from more than one of her relatives.

"He released her," Gianna repeated. "And it worked."

For the first time in her entire life she heard Primo swear. She was so shocked she could only sit and stare, openmouthed. Her grandfather spared Sev a brief, sorrowful look. "It pains me to say this about my own son, but Dominic lied."

Gianna shook her head. "No. No, he didn't. He left after that and Aunt Laura called a friend. She said that The Inferno was gone. She said she felt it leave when Uncle Dominic released her. And she was glad. Glad The Inferno couldn't force her to love someone against her will any longer. Now she could go sailing with him in the morning while they discussed the divorce and it wouldn't interfere with her decisions." Gianna started to cry. "I'm sorry. I never wanted to tell any of you this because you were all so happy. Now I've ruined it for everyone."

Constantine swept her into his arms and cradled her close. "Shh, *piccola*. You haven't ruined anything."

"Yes, I have. I released you. The Inferno is gone. You won't love me now."

"Is it gone?" he asked tenderly. "All this time I have been sitting here listening to your story and my palm has itched and throbbed just as it always has. Even more important…" He took a deep breath. "I have never in my life told a woman I loved her. I've even resisted saying it to you. Pride, I suppose. A last defense against something beyond my control."

She fought to free herself from his hold, but he wouldn't let her go. "You don't want to love me, do you?"

"I don't want to be controlled by love," he corrected. "So much of my life was spent being controlled by others, by circumstance, by my family's financial difficulties, that I fought what cannot be fought. What I wasn't willing to admit until this moment is that love doesn't mean surrendering control." He looked at her then, his dark eyes filled with an emotion impossible to mistake. "It means surrendering your heart into the safekeeping of someone you love and trust more than anyone else in the world. And that I do freely. *Ti amo, piccola.* I love you."

Helpless tears flowed down her cheeks. "I don't understand. I took away The Inferno."

He laced their hands together. "Stop and feel with your heart. Is it still there, or not?"

Her breath caught. Yes. Yes, it was. She didn't understand it. She stared in wonder at their linked hands. "I still feel it. How is that possible? I released you."

Sev crouched in front of her. "Gianna, you should have told us this long ago. We would have explained the truth." Pain ripped through his gaze. "My parents never felt The Inferno for each other. My father married my mother for her fortune, not because he loved her. He loved another woman, Cara Moretti. *She* was his Inferno soul mate."

"But Aunt Laura said she felt The Inferno."

Sev's mouth compressed. "I'm sure Mamma thought she did. Though Babbo never loved her, not the way she deserved. That didn't change the fact that she adored him. I think she wanted to feel The Inferno. So she convinced herself she did. But it wasn't true."

In all the years since her thirteenth birthday, not once had Gianna ever considered the possibility that her uncle had lied to her aunt. That he could have done such an awful thing to his wife. But he had. Considering how hard the knowledge hit her, it had to be far worse for Sev. Impulsively she threw her arms around his neck and wrapped him up in a fierce hug.

"I'm sorry. I'm so, so sorry."

He patted her back. "I already knew most of it," he reassured her. "I didn't realize he'd used The Inferno to convince my mother to marry him. But it isn't that big of a surprise, considering some of the other things he's done."

The information had also hit Primo and Nonna hard, particularly her grandmother. But there had always been a steely strength buried beneath Nonna's sweetness. "This is a happy occasion, not a sad one," she informed her family. "We are finished here, yes? It is time for the wedding."

"No," Constantine said. His hands slid from Gianna's shoulders and he stood, folding his arms across his chest. "We're not getting married. Not yet."

Gianna rose and spun to face him, panic flaring to life. "Constantine?"

"You released me. That suggests you wanted to be released, too."

Her panic grew, breaking across her in great, messy waves. "No. No, that's not true."

"Then why release me?"

She took a step in his direction. "Don't you understand? I don't want you to marry me because you're honor-bound. I don't want you to marry me because of The Inferno. I want you to love me." Her voice broke and it took her a moment to gather herself sufficiently to speak again. "I want you to love *me*. Just me."

Constantine closed his eyes. He reached for her hand and before she could guess his intentions, slipped her engagement ring from her finger. Her entire family stiffened. Francesca gasped, while Ariana murmured a broken, "Oh, no." He ignored them all.

"Have you never once looked at your ring?"

Gianna stared in horror. "You mean take it off? Before we were married?"

"Of course I mean take it off," he said in exasperation.

"Oh, no. It's bad luck," the women chimed in, practically in unison.

He released a sigh. "Got it. Well, I chose it very, very carefully. Sev can attest to that."

Her cousin nodded. "It took hours. He must have gone through every ring in the entire Eternity line before he settled on this one," he informed her.

Constantine nodded. "That's because all the rings have names. It's part of what makes them so special. I needed one with the perfect name." He tilted it so she could see the tiny script inside the band. "Read what it says."

She needed a moment to blink the tears away. The letters swam into focus, forming words. *Before All Else...Love.* Then she was crying again. "Do you really mean it?"

"I really mean it, *piccola*. Honor means everything to me, you know this. But you... You are my heart and soul." He returned the ring to her finger, this time with an attitude of permanence. "You are not Laura and I am not Dominic. It's our love that makes this marriage honorable. Without it, there would be no honor in the vows we take."

Gianna flung herself into Constantine's embrace. "I was afraid you'd feel trapped. That one day you'd resent me."

His arms closed around her like iron bands. "Do you remember my telling you that I don't like taking off my shoes, not even when I relax?"

"Yes."

"There's a reason for that." He spared her family a brief shamed look before his gaze settled on his sister, Ariana.

Gianna saw compassion in his sister's expression, along with understanding. "Growing up, there was no money. My grandmother Penelope helped out the best she could, but it wasn't nearly enough, not for an estate the size of ours. Do you know how we survived?"

Gianna shook her head.

"My father traded on the Romano name." Considering Constantine's pride, it must have been the most difficult thing he'd ever admitted. "We lived off the charity of others, including the d'Angelos. We sold our illustrious heritage and scintillating company for the bread we ate and the beds we slept in. For loans that were never repaid."

"That's why you wouldn't come to me empty-handed."

He nodded. "And that's why I don't take off my shoes."

She frowned in confusion. "I don't understand."

"Our visits didn't always end well," he explained gently. "When they didn't, we soon learned to be ready to leave at a moment's notice. Fleeing into a cold winter night without shoes is a memorable experience. You learn very quickly not to make the same mistake twice."

"Oh, Constantine," she whispered.

He set her aside and toed off first one shoe, then the other. Crossing to the window, he opened it and tossed his shoes outside. Then he returned to her. "You are all I want. All I'll ever want. Do you understand now, *piccola*?" He cupped her face between his Infernoed hands and kissed her with all the pent-up passion he possessed. "I don't need to keep my shoes close by because I'm finally home. This is where I belong and I'm here to stay. My sense of honor bound me to you. Our love is what will keep us together."

Primo rose to his feet. *"Salute! Alla famiglia!"*

The rest of the family picked up the cheer while Constantine swept his bride into his arms. As one they exited the room in a grand procession to the chapel, laughing and crying, their happiness spilling out in great joyous waves over those assembled in the church. Down the aisle they came.

They were Dantes. *La famiglia.* And that said it all.

One Inferno family.

One Inferno heart.

Soul mates found.

Soul mates bonded—united for all time.

* * * * *

Don't miss Day Leclaire's next Desire
THE BILLIONAIRE'S BABY SURPRISE

COMING NEXT MONTH

Available June 14, 2011

HDCNM0511

REQUEST YOUR FREE BOOKS!
2 FREE NOVELS PLUS 2 FREE GIFTS!

ALWAYS POWERFUL, PASSIONATE AND PROVOCATIVE

YES! Please send me 2 FREE Harlequin Desire® novels and my 2 FREE gifts (gifts are worth about $10). After receiving them, if I don't wish to receive any more books, I can return the shipping statement marked "cancel." If I don't cancel, I will receive 6 brand-new novels every month and be billed just $4.05 per book in the U.S. or $4.74 per book in Canada. That's a saving of at least 15% off the cover price! It's quite a bargain! Shipping and handling is just 50¢ per book in the U.S. and 75¢ per book in Canada.* I understand that accepting the 2 free books and gifts places me under no obligation to buy anything. I can always return a shipment and cancel at any time. Even if I never buy another book, the two free books and gifts are mine to keep forever.

225/326 SDN FC65

Name _____ (PLEASE PRINT)

Address _____ Apt. #

City _____ State/Prov. _____ Zip/Postal Code

Signature (if under 18, a parent or guardian must sign)

Mail to the **Reader Service:**
IN U.S.A.: P.O. Box 1867, Buffalo, NY 14240-1867
IN CANADA: P.O. Box 609, Fort Erie, Ontario L2A 5X3

Not valid for current subscribers to Harlequin Desire books.

Want to try two free books from another line?
Call 1-800-873-8635 or visit www.ReaderService.com.

* Terms and prices subject to change without notice. Prices do not include applicable taxes. Sales tax applicable in N.Y. Canadian residents will be charged applicable taxes. Offer not valid in Quebec. This offer is limited to one order per household. All orders subject to credit approval. Credit or debit balances in a customer's account(s) may be offset by any other outstanding balance owed by or to the customer. Please allow 4 to 6 weeks for delivery. Offer available while quantities last.

Your Privacy—The Reader Service is committed to protecting your privacy. Our Privacy Policy is available online at www.ReaderService.com or upon request from the Reader Service.

We make a portion of our mailing list available to reputable third parties that offer products we believe may interest you. If you prefer that we not exchange your name with third parties, or if you wish to clarify or modify your communication preferences, please visit us at www.ReaderService.com/consumerschoice or write to us at Reader Service Preference Service, P.O. Box 9062, Buffalo, NY 14269. Include your complete name and address.

HDES11

"THANKS FOR NOT TURNING ON THE LIGHTS," Tyler said. "I'm a mess."

"Not in my book." Even in low light, Alex had a good view of her yellow shirt plastered to her body. It was all he could do not to reach for her, mud and all. But the next move needed to be hers, not his.

She slicked her wet hair back and squeezed some water out of the ends as she glanced upward. "I like the sound of the rain on a tin roof."

"Me, too."

She met his gaze briefly and looked away. "Where's the sink?"

"At the far end, beyond the last stall."

Tyler's running shoes squished as she walked down the aisle between the rows of stalls. She glanced sideways at Alex. "So how much of a cowboy are you these days? Do you ride the range and stuff?"

"I ride." He liked being able to say that. "Why?"

"Just wondered. Last summer, you were still a city boy. You even told me you weren't the cowboy type, but you're…different now."

He wasn't sure if that was a good thing or a bad thing. Maybe she preferred city boys to cowboys. "How am I different?"

"Well, you dress differently, and your hair's a little longer. Your face seems a little more chiseled, but maybe that's because of your hair. Also, there's something else, something harder to define, an attitude…"

"Are you saying I have an attitude?"

"Not in a bad way. It's more like a quiet confidence."

He was flattered, but still he had to laugh. "I just admitted a while ago that I have all kinds of doubts about this event tomorrow. That doesn't seem like quiet confidence to me."

"This isn't about your job, it's about…your…" She took a deep breath. "It's about your sex appeal, okay? I have no business talking about it, because it will only make me want to do things I shouldn't do." She started toward the end of the barn. "Now, where's that sink? We need to get cleaned up and go back to the house. Dinner is probably ready, and I—"

He spun her around and pulled her into his arms, mud and all. "Let's do those things." Then he kissed her, knowing that she would kiss him back, knowing that this time he would take that kiss where he wanted it to go. And she would let him.

Follow Tyler and Alex's wild adventures in
SHOULD'VE BEEN A COWBOY
Available June 2011 only from Harlequin® Blaze™
wherever books are sold.